Tempting Love on Holly Lane

(Island County #5)

KARICE BOLTON

ISBN-13: 978-1539397380

ISBN-10: 1539397386

Chapter One

I looked around my tiny cabin and pure joy filled me to the brim. I was in the middle of nowhere with an acre of trees surrounding me. My cozy cottage—as I'd aptly named it—was a one-bedroom beauty in need of lots of work, but the bones offered amazing potential, or so the real estate agent promised me. I'd bought it from an older man who wanted to retire to Arizona so he could be closer to his daughter and her children.

I scanned the great room, which was empty and opened to a kitchen reminiscent of the seventies, complete with lime green wallpaper, where only a few boxes had been piled in the far corner along with my mp3 player placed gingerly on top.

This was the life!

No honking horns to wake me up at five in the morning or neighbors pounding on a thin wall, screaming to turn down the television.

I shimmied over to the front door to prop it open and peeked my head outside. A light dusting of snow covered the ground, but I'd somehow managed to overheat my little cabin with the wood fireplace, and I was dying even with the windows open. I couldn't wait until the television got hooked up, but until then, I'd get to blast my music all weekend.

On that last thought, I grabbed the remote to my stereo and turned it on. I had a whole can of paint and a half-bottle of wine to get through tonight, and I was more than willing to complete both missions in a timely manner.

I took off my hoodie, poured myself glass number one, and opened the can of white paint as the theme song to *Flashdance* filled my little home.

My first DIY project was to paint the paneling in the great room. I twisted my blonde hair into a ponytail, tugged on my oversized tank top, and dipped the brush in the paint as Irene Cara told me to take my passion and make it happen, but before I could do that, I needed to turn up the stereo a little louder just because I could.

I'd escaped Manhattan!

A little twinge of sadness surfaced, but I quickly pushed it out of my head. Things happened for a reason, and I was meant to come to Fireweed Island to help my sister with her tea shop.

The synthesizer rattled the floor as I brushed the first stroke of white paint over the paneling, and I felt the music lift me up. It had been so long since I'd let music blast without a care in the world.

What had it been? Since college?

Once the brush ran out of paint, I took a sip of my red wine and reloaded. I kept *What a Feeling* on repeat and let the eighties music take me to my happy place. It wasn't until I got halfway down the wall that I realized my little cabin was only getting hotter. The wood fireplace was really going to save on heating bills, but in the meantime, I had to figure out a way to cool off. I yanked my tank over my head and tossed it on the mustard-colored carpet and took a swig of my wine as the music pumped up my little space.

By the time I'd finished my second glass of wine, I'd started painting hearts on the wall and kept dancing like I was actually in *Flashdance*, and it never felt so good.

. . . until a sexy, masculine voice interrupted my last move.

"Excuse me. Was there a party on this street that I wasn't invited to?" A man's smooth voice echoed over the eighties soundtrack.

Covering the front of my bra with my free arm, I spun around in a blazing fury and held my paintbrush as a weapon between the man and myself.

But the moment I saw the guy at my door, I became nearly speechless at how good-looking he was in a rugged, cocky, so-not-my-type kind of way.

Great! I landed a nosy, albeit hot, lumberjack as a neighbor.

His gorgeous brown eyes connected with mine, and I felt a current run through my body, which was a really obnoxious reaction, considering I was standing here in a pair of ratty jeans and a bra.

"Who do you think you are, coming into my house?" I yelled over Irene Cara, waving the paintbrush at him.

"I'm technically not in your house." He tapped the doorframe, and a piece of wood fell off.

The story of my life.

He looked down at the wood before picking it up and grinning.

"Glad you find it funny that my house is falling apart all around me." My brow arched as I kept my elbow bent in front of me to cover up the red lace separating all of me from Mr. Sexy. "The new door I picked out is in my garage. I just haven't had time to hang it."

"I don't find that funny at all." He smirked. "But I do find a woman dancing to *What a Feeling* on repeat for the last three hours . . . funny." His eyes glinted with intrigue, and I couldn't help the flutter that erupted deep in my belly.

I grabbed the remote from the floor and turned the music down a few clicks before turning to face him again.

"It hasn't been three hours," I corrected, trying to hide my smile. "Can you toss me that hoodie by your foot?"

"That would require me stepping over the threshold. That okay with you?" His brow quirked and I bit my lip, nodding. "And it *was* three hours. I know because after the first hour, I couldn't imagine that anyone could stomach it for one second longer."

He shoved up the sleeve of his red plaid flannel shirt, and I couldn't help but notice how muscular his bronzed forearm was as he bent over. His shirt molded perfectly across his wide shoulders and tight back muscles, which led to his lean, muscular legs that his jeans did a terrible job of hiding. I held in a sigh. Men certainly didn't exist like this where I'd come from. The male species back there were more in-line with the wiry and pale variety from spending all day in skyscrapers.

He picked up the hoodie and tossed it over about a foot away from me before flashing a wry grin. He stood up and his dark hair fell over his brow.

"Nice aim, *playboy*." I didn't know if it was the wine or the new town, but I let my arm fall to my side before picking up my hoodie, and I watched the guy's jaw nearly drop to the ground. "You're welcome." I winked, slid on my hoodie, and zipped it up.

"Wow. So you're my new neighbor?" He took a step back as if I'd bite him, and who knew? Maybe I would.

This move was full of new beginnings.

"Sure am." I bent over and reached for my glass of wine, correcting a little wobble as I stood back up and took a sip, watching him carefully. "You thirsty?"

"Nah. I'm good. I should probably head back. I have a pretty big order I'm working on."

I kept my eyes on him and took another sip but noticed he wasn't leaving.

"Welcome to State Road 26, neighbor." He raked his fingers through his brown hair while trying really hard to keep his eyes on mine.

"Thank you." I hid a smile.

He took in a deep breath and glanced at my fireplace, his eyes widening. "Shit. Your woodstove is overfired."

"Huh?" I asked, watching him dash over to the fireplace and adjust some dial on the front of it. He stayed kneeling in front of the flames, waiting for something. "Did this come with a manual?"

"No." My brows furrowed as I thought about where one might be. "Is everything okay?"

He stood up slowly and turned around. "You almost burned your house down, but other than that, I'd say your night's going spectacularly well."

"Are you serious?" A cold chill blasted through my veins as I looked at the fireplace.

"Yeah. You had the draft control on the 'high burn' setting, which is fine for heating up a cold room, but you want to adjust back to low or the stove will overfire."

"What can happen then?" My pulse spiked.

"The fire burns too hot and can actually melt metal parts on the fireplace." He bit his lip and glanced over my shoulder.

"Wow. Thank you. I can't believe . . ." I followed his gaze to the only open box in the room and gasped.

He started laughing, and I ran to the box to block his view.

"That is a neck massager. My sister just brought it over." I huffed and attempted to secure the flaps of the box. "I've been tense since the move."

"Is that what they call them now?" He walked up behind me, and I swore I could nearly sense the testosterone rolling off him.

I couldn't help but laugh. The truth was that it actually was a neck and shoulder massager. Working in front of a computer screen for so many years had made my shoulders and neck a tight mess, but it was shaped oddly.

"It just so happens that the shape is misleading. My chiropractor in New York recommended this brand, and it works wonders."

"I bet it does." His smile was infectious. "But I thought your sister brought it over."

"I swear. It isn't what it looks like."

"Then why'd you run to the box so quickly?"

"Because I *know* what it looks like, and so far, you've managed to see a very different side of me. I didn't want you to get the wrong idea."

"You mean you don't always dance to eighties tunes in a red bra while drinking wine and painting?"

"Nope. First time."

"I don't know that I believe that."

"I used to live in Manhattan in an apartment the size of the kitchen. Cranking my music is a luxury." I sucked on my lip for a split second, and his eyes dropped to my mouth, sending electricity through my veins.

"And the dancing in a bra part?" he asked, his voice lowered.

"Well, that might not be an anomaly," I confessed, grinning.

He sucked in a deep breath.

I liked that I caught him off-guard. It had been a long time since . . . well, since anything.

"Finding you in a bra isn't as fun as finding Frank in one." He chuckled, his eyes staying on mine. "True story."

"No way." I shook my head. "I don't believe it. Frank? As in previous owner, Frank?"

He shrugged, a wry grin spreading across his lips.

"I don't believe you." I narrowed my eyes on my neighbor and stuck my hand out to distract myself from the chemistry I was feeling. "Holly Wildes."

"Nice to meet you, Holly. I'm Nick Boren." His smile nearly undid me as his hand left mine.

"Well, thank you for saving my house from burning down." I cleared my throat. "But I have to get back to painting my living room."

"Sure you do." He nodded and glanced at the box with the neck massager.

"Do you usually spend your Friday nights spying on your neighbors?" I crossed my arms.

"Only the attractive ones." Nick's charm might

work on the island girls, but not me. I'd been fooled one too many times by the arrogant males of Manhattan.

"Well, Frank *was* a silver fox," I concluded. "I can see how he kept your attention."

Nick's laughter filled my small cabin and my heart, which was quite disconcerting. I came to Fireweed Island to get away from people, not welcome them in, especially ones like Nick.

"He actually was," Nick agreed, slowly making his way to the door. "You know, we're expecting a snowstorm this weekend."

I rolled my eyes. "Four inches isn't exactly what I'd call a blizzard."

His grin widened. "Maybe not in New York, but here it's a different story. You have plenty of wood, food, water?"

"I'd say so." My brows furrowed. "Why do you ask?"

"When a storm like this hits so early in the season, the power tends to go out, and the roads are generally not where you'd want to spend any time. I once got stuck on 405 for five hours because traffic came to a standstill once the snow started falling."

From four inches of snow?

"I'm sure I'll be just fine, but thank you for worrying about me." I smiled.

"I'm not worried. I just don't want to have to haul you and your shiny red Fiat out of a ditch somewhere." He held up the piece of wood from my door. "I'll come back tomorrow to fix this. Have a nice night daydreaming about becoming a stripper, Holly."

"That isn't what *Flashdance* is about," I called after him.

Nick waved behind him as he trekked down my driveway, and it wasn't until he was out of view that I realized I hadn't taken a breath since he'd left.

Chapter Two

"Can you believe he thinks *Flashdance* is about stripping?" I looked over at my sister, Maddie, who was busy filling one of the tins with mint tea.

Maddie glanced over her shoulder and grinned. "I'm not sure that was the point he was trying to make." She chuckled. "You were painting and gyrating in your bra."

I placed my hands on my hips and cocked my head. "In my own living room. Besides, I was overheating, and I didn't want to ruin a perfectly good hoodie with paint."

Maddie slid the tin back on the shelf and turned to face me. Her hair was a darker blonde than mine and her eyes sparkled blue. Mine were brown.

"Nonetheless, you were dancing your heart

out and caressing a paintbrush with your front door wide open. You live on one acre, Holly, not a thirty-acre pasture. Believe it or not, sound still carries." She grinned and shook her head. "You always have a knack."

"How so?"

"Remember Donald?"

I cringed. How could I forget Donald? He was the Resident Assistant (RA) on our floor of the dorm back in college. He requested a quick dorm transfer after walking in on me singing and dancing in the shower. I couldn't hear him hollering for an "all-clear", and he couldn't hear me singing in the back where the showers were located. I hadn't realized that in all my singing glory, I'd managed to sweep the shower curtain open and Donald got an eyeful. I wasn't in the most flattering of positions, and I'd scarred him for life. For some reason, he switched from a science major to history after that and always turned beet red when he saw me on campus.

"I just need to be a little more cautious at the house. I guess I got overly excited that I no longer had to ride an elevator to an apartment or shut the curtains to change."

"Correction. You should still shut your curtains to change." Maddie laughed. "See? I think you just set yourself up."

"If it means getting to meet more Nicks, I'm all for it." I wiped down the shelves and looked out the window to see a road full of cars. "Is it always this busy on Main Street on a Saturday?"

"A storm is coming." She shut down her

laptop.

"But there's no snow yet. Why's the traffic so crazy?" I asked.

"People are stocking up. Do you have candles and flashlights?"

I shook my head.

"Well, I'd swing by the store and pick some up."

"Seriously?"

"You'll see."

I rolled my eyes. "Worrywart. Now tell me what you know about Nick."

"Besides that he's one of the most gorgeous men to walk the planet?"

"You think so too?" I asked.

"I think all the women on and off Fireweed think that."

"Is he involved with anyone?" My pulse was starting to quicken and I had no idea why.

"Well . . ." My sister's brows pulled together and she looked conflicted.

"Oh. My. God. You two are? I'm so sorry. I'll totally—"

"Not even." My sister grabbed her jacket and scarf off the hook behind her. "Come on. We're shutting down early. It's a snow day."

"But there's no snow."

"Just wait." She winked as I put my coat on. "Anyway, about Nick. It's not that he's involved with just one person. He's more of a . . ."

"Player?" I finished for my sister.

"Yes. He's definitely a player. That is the perfect adjective to describe Nick and the perfect one to keep me far away."

"What's he do for a living?" I followed my sister out the door and waited as she locked it. The idea of getting to know a player didn't sound all bad to me, especially since I was in no way ready for any kind of commitment.

It was early November, and since I'd arrived on the island, the weather wavered between rain and fog with a dusting of snow here and there. Orange and yellow chrysanthemums lined the sidewalk and dried leaves littered the soil and streets. There was no doubt about it. Fireweed was a beautiful place to live, even if they were inept at preparing for snow.

"He builds custom furniture, but I think he's been doing more design work lately and someone else is building it. Or maybe not. I really don't know. It's hard to keep track of everyone around here." Her fingers wiggled in the air.

"That's cool. Then he knows how to use his hands." I flashed a smile and Maddie groaned.

"He tends to avoid most women on the island."

"What do you mean?" I asked.

She shrugged. "It's just something I've noticed. I've never seen him with anyone from Fireweed besides his friends. The women he's with all seem to be from the mainland."

"He's worth a ferry trip?" My brow arched.

"Apparently so, or he just doesn't want to anger the female population of Fireweed."

A blast of frigid air sent a chill through me.

"Smart man." I nodded. "It's a small place to

live."

"And so it begins," Maddie said as I zipped my coat up. "It even smells like snow."

She was obviously done talking about Nick. I loved my sister to pieces, but when she was through with a conversation, she just turned it off and carried on. It was a habit I learned about long ago.

"I'm looking forward to seeing what all the fuss is about." I had to admit the temperature had dropped tremendously since I arrived at my sister's tea shop, and the crispness in the air was almost painful.

"Promise me you'll get some basic supplies. The islands are notorious for losing power."

"Things to tell your sister before convincing her to move to an island clear across the country," I teased. "But yes, I promise to get some supplies on the way home."

"You could always stay at my house for the weekend."

"And relive the magical moments from when I first moved out here? I don't think so." My sister was sweet, but she was also extremely rigid. She woke up every day at the same time and her schedule never veered off course, which is why a snow day kind of surprised me. I'd never imagine her shutting down shop when the store hours are clearly stated.

"Why are you smiling?" my sister asked as we walked to our cars.

"No reason."

"Come on. Don't make me pull it out of you."

She studied me closely from the corner of her eye.

"You just usually like to play by the rules. I'm surprised you're shutting down the shop early."

"You'll see soon enough."

I gave my sister a quick hug and climbed into my Fiat. I really wasn't looking forward to spending any time without power, but at least I'd be warm with my fireplace.

I popped my car into reverse and waved at my sister before heading to the grocery store down the street. When I turned into the parking lot I was in shock at how packed it was. I didn't see an empty parking spot anywhere, and people were pushing carts full of supplies like there was a run on common sense.

I circled the lot a few times and finally nabbed a spot next to the door.

See? Luck was already on my side.

Since all the carts were taken, I went inside, grabbed a small basket, and immediately stood in line for a pumpkin spice latte. First things first. As I waited for my turn, I watched the frantic movements of moms, husbands, and children running around and putting all kinds of things in their carts. Whether it was marshmallows, cookies, or potato chips, nothing that was going into the carts looked absolutely life or death.

I ordered my drink and waited for it to be called as I realized this snowstorm was calling out for one big party of corn chips and salsa. I might throw in a flashlight or candles, but the necessities weren't what drove people to shop. It was getting to eat junk food and spend time with the family that made these aisles full.

Taking a sip of the sweetness, I made my way down the aisles, tossing in cookies, chips, soda, canned soup, and batteries. It wasn't until I found the aisle where candles and flashlights were supposed to be that I realized things were going to be very dark this weekend if the power did go out. I guess in between tossing in potato chips and graham crackers, the islanders managed to snag all the candles too.

I let out a huff and wandered to the checkout and stood in line for what seemed like hours. It wasn't until a woman a few carts behind me started giggling that I came out of my trance.

"What I wouldn't give to spend a snowy weekend all alone with him." The woman chuckled, and I glanced behind me to see a woman talking into her phone as if we were all a part of her conversation. "The way he works that wood. Could you imagine what he'd—"

"Excuse me," the woman behind me told the sex fiend as she covered her son's ears. "Not all of us need to hear what your weekend plans are."

"Oh, Mrs. Lachtes, I only wish he were part of my weekend plans." She hung up on whoever was on the other end of the phone and grinned at the woman behind me.

These two knew each other?

"Regardless, the whole store doesn't need to hear about your Nick fantasies." The mom removed her hands from her son's ears and tried to hide a smile while I stood frozen. They were talking about my neighbor?

"I never said it was Nick whom I was referring to," the other woman nearly stuttered.

"You didn't have to. We all know."

Nick really was at the tip of all single women's thoughts.

Figured.

"That's so not true," the grinning woman countered.

"How many other woodworkers on this island do women talk about?" the mom teased. I realized these two were good friends, but I was so immersed in learning about Nick, I didn't realize the checker had already rung me up.

"Miss?"

I spun around and apologized as I quickly inserted my debit card, still keeping an ear open to the conversation behind me.

"Even if I camped out at his house, he wouldn't look in my direction. He's too good for the locals." I caught her rolling her eyes.

"I don't think that's it at all. Can you imagine the hassle if he started dating here? He runs through females like there's no tomorrow."

"Have a nice day, and stay safe from the storm," the checker told me, handing me a paper bag of groceries and scooting me on out of the line.

I waltzed to my car, shoved my junk food on the backseat, and took off toward home. At least living across the street from the island's player would give me some entertainment. It might be fun to see who rolls out of his house each morning.

I turned down the long road winding to my driveway and happened to look across the street at Nick's house. Actually, I couldn't really see his house, only a workshop along the drive canopied by giant Douglas firs and naked maples, but I did spot his truck in his driveway, which provided an unexpected giddiness.

Pulling into my own driveway, I was shocked to see two sawhorses in front of my cabin with lumber stretched between, and an extremely handsome man running a saw down one of the boards.

I turned off my ignition, grabbed the groceries from the backseat, and hopped out of the car. The sound of the buzzing saw echoed through the air. He obviously didn't hear my car come up behind him. Not wanting to startle him into slicing off a finger, I stood behind Nick, waiting for him to finish.

My mind was running rampant with different scenarios and imagining how tonight could end. It didn't help the rumors around town as he worked in front of me with his bare arms flexing and moving the saw along the wood, putting all kinds of thoughts into my brain about what else he was good at.

Nick took a step back and lopped off another chunk of wood, and the definition in his forearms uncorked something completely screwy in me. I'd never been turned on by manual labor, and that was essentially what was happening here.

It was freezing outside, and he was only

wearing a navy t-shirt, loose-fitting jeans, and a leather tool belt. He had flecks of sawdust in his hair, and I had an overwhelming desire to ruffle them out for him.

This was crazy!

He took a step back and turned off the saw, and my heart literally skipped a beat as I watched him take one of the boards up the steps to the vacant hole where the front door used to be.

Things really were different on Fireweed.

I cleared my throat—trying to get up enough nerve to thank him—when he spun around, his eyes connecting with mine. I shifted the grocery bag from one hip to the other.

"You're home early." A huge grin spread across his lips and my heart flipped.

How did he know my schedule? Had he been paying attention?

"Am I?"

He grabbed the drill and put in a couple of screws before placing it back down.

"I was only teasing about tearing my house apart. You didn't have to do this." I walked up the steps and scanned the work zone.

"I felt bad," he said, stepping aside to allow me into my home. "And I thought this was a better way to welcome you to the neighborhood than telling you to turn down the music."

"I didn't know you were telling me to turn down the music." I chuckled. "Do you always hang doors for your neighbors?" I stepped inside my freezing house.

"First time." He kept his eyes on me, and for some reason, the attention nearly unfastened me as I set the bag on the kitchen counter.

How could he produce these feelings with just a look?

"Well, thank you." I studied him, wondering if it was true that he always stayed away from island women.

Maybe it was worth the move to Seattle.

He rubbed the dark whiskers along his jaw and nodded.

"It's the least I can do. You've got your hands full with this place. Anyway, your door frame was completely rotten, and I happened to have some wood, so. . ."

My smile widened as I saw a flush along his neck and cheeks, but it vanished as fast as it came. I had to have imagined it.

"Would you like anything to eat while you finish? I took your and my sister's advice about preparing for the storm."

"Is that so?" He wandered over to me and peeked into the bag.

Just being close to him was a turn-on.

"Fudge-striped cookies and BBQ potato chips are your way of preparing for a storm?" he said, laughing.

"And the rest of the island's way, from what I saw." I grinned, taking both packages out of the bag.

"What about things like flashlights, candles, batteries?" He glanced over at the box from the day before. "Although something tells me you have plenty of batteries."

I ignored him and grabbed the chicken noodle soup out of the bag.

"For your information, they were out of the basics, and I'd rather be full in the dark than hungry in the dark. Would you like some cookies?" I asked, ripping the container open before he responded.

"I'm good. I should get back at it." He pointed at the door, and I smiled before taking a bite of the fudge-striped goodness.

"I feel so bad. You've got to let me repay you somehow. How about I make you dinner one night?"

Something changed behind his expression and his eyes dropped to the ugly carpet. "You don't owe me a thing. It's just a neighbor being friendly with a neighbor."

"But—" My heart fell. I guess it was true about him and island girls.

He held up his hand and a smile crept along his lips. "Just let me catch you dancing sometime, and all will be well in my world."

"Speaking of which, do you think it's fair you saw me without a shirt and I haven't seen you sans clothing?"

Complete shock flashed across his face, and I had to admit, I was equally as surprised at what tumbled out of my mouth.

I was enjoying this new me.

"Umm. It's like thirty degrees." His brow arched slightly.

I shrugged, hiding my smile as I began putting

away the groceries. It had been worth a shot.

The high-powered drill sounded again, and I glanced up to see Nick.

...without his shirt.

I gasped, and he glanced in my direction, grinning and shaking his head, as I kept myself upright with the help of the kitchen counter.

The carved definition of his arms had nothing on his abs and pecs. His bronzed skin was molded over ripped muscles and tight abs, impossible for most mere mortals to obtain. Yet here he was, standing in my entry, and there wasn't a thing I could do about it.

As he stretched to secure a few more screws, his obliques lengthened, and I thought about how they would feel under my fingertips. The drilling stopped, and I brought my eyes to Nick's.

"You okay over there?" he asked, feigning innocence.

"Totally fine," I muttered. "Aren't you cold?"

"Not in the least bit." He flashed another grin, and I knew I was in trouble.

Chapter Three

Sure enough, the snow began coming down around seven at night and the power went out by eight. Nick had finished hanging the door before it got dark, and I'd managed to get the house toasty warm once he'd left.

The new door was the perfect addition for my cozy little cabin. It was light pine and had a little window at the top. My goal was to trim all the windows and doors in my house with the same light pine.

To be honest, I was still in shock that Nick hung my front door. It was such a nice thing for him to do, especially for no reason.

I'd found the door on sale after I'd first signed the papers on my house, but I had absolutely no idea how to actually replace it, and after watching Nick, I was glad I didn't attempt it on my own.

Wouldn't it figure I live across from a hot, handy neighbor who only dates women who live thirty-plus miles away?

I tugged on my flannel snowflake pajamas and let out a sigh while I stared at the flames in the fireplace, which produced the only source of light for the house. I'd carted my sleeping bag into the great room and piled the floor with pillows.

I couldn't wait until the carpet was replaced next week. The installers would be here with the hickory floors I'd picked out on the mainland, and the biggest change to my cabin would be complete.

I didn't want to buy any furniture until the floors were done because I figured trying to move everything would be impossible, and I had no real place to store the stuff anyway.

My mind kept looping with all the quiet and I groaned as my to-do list kept circulating.

I had a lengthy list of items I wanted to get taken care of before my parents came out over Thanksgiving. I think they were still in shock I'd left Manhattan. Some days, I was still in shock that I no longer had to hurry to get dressed, slam a coffee, and make my way into the office by eight. I wish I could say I'd left a ton of friends behind and that it was a tough choice to move across the country, but the truth was that I didn't leave much behind at all.

I'd spent so many years trying to get ahead at the investment firm that it left very little time for friendships or relationships of any kind.

But my parents didn't know that. My mom and dad only knew of the parties I'd attend all nights of the week, how I was rarely ever at my tiny apartment, and how much I loved the city.

The truth was that the parties were networking and client functions—mostly put on by my firm—and the reason I wasn't at my apartment very often was because I buried myself in work at the office. And as for the city? On the rare moments that I got to enjoy Manhattan, I found Manhattan to be lively and full of people watching.

A shiver ran down my spine at the sudden isolation that seeped into my bones just as a flash of headlights bounced off my wall. I hopped up and glanced out the window to see Nick's truck pulling out of his driveway. About four or five inches of snow had already piled on the ground and the white stuff was still falling.

I wondered where Nick was going. Not that it mattered . . .

But it was such a wet snow, and I now fully understood all the cause for concern. Icicles already dangled from my gutters, and the heaviness of the snow was what most likely pulled down the electricity. Yet Nick was headed out with more snow on the way.

I shrugged to myself and wandered over to the kitchen counter, where I'd left my Kindle. The orange glow of the fire didn't quite reach the kitchen, so finding exactly where I put the chips was a bit more challenging. Rather than bother with a bowl, I grabbed the bag and made my way back into the family room.

I began reading the mystery I'd started on the night before, but I quickly changed my mind. Considering how many parallels the main character had with me at the moment, I reconsidered what genre I needed.

Lights out.

Storm brewing.

And completely isolated and cut off from the rest of the world.

Another shiver ran down my spine, and I groaned as I picked a nice and light time-travel romance instead of the mystery.

I'd gotten several chapters in and half-a-bag down on the chips when I saw Nick's lights brighten my room again, which was odd. I stood up and watched him back into his driveway. I saw a shadow of someone with a ponytail sitting in the passenger seat, and my stomach tightened immediately.

He'd go out in a blizzard to find a woman for the night when there was a perfectly willing and waiting one across the street?

Hmph.

I moved to the side of the window and peered out, hoping the beige drapes would hide most of my body, while I watched the truck stop and his door swing wide open. The snow must be too deep to try to reverse any further into the driveway.

Hopefully, his floozy wore appropriate shoes for the hike to his house. I giggled at the thought of whoever she was falling face forward into the snow.

A purely evil thought.

No. I wasn't that cruel. This guy had his life already established before I moved here, and I was just jealous that I wasn't the one with him. No biggie.

But I squinted my eyes to see better and felt a flutter of excitement when movement began. I was curious to see what kind of woman Nick fell for. The snowflakes slowed to a stop, making it easier for spying.

It felt like I was on some covert mission as I watched the other door open. My heart began hammering in my chest and my palms became damp with anticipation. I watched the woman's arms waving in the air as she attempted to stabilize herself with each step forward in the slippery snow, and I secretly hoped my dream of her face-planting came to life.

The moon bounced against the white of the snow, making it far too easy to see the appeal of Nick even in the heart of darkness, and I let out a deep grunt.

It had been far too long since I'd been attracted to someone. Maybe he wasn't really all that great, and I was just in a drought or something.

Such wishful thinking.

He was dressed in the same jeans as earlier, but now he had on a heavy, dark sweater and a matching knit cap. Nick reached back into the cab of the truck and pulled out a puffy coat and my chest tightened. I wasn't supposed to be paying attention to him. I was supposed to be checking her out.

I was such a horrible person for spying on my hot neighbor. He glanced in my direction and I stiffened along the drapery. There was no way he'd be able to see my silhouette with just the glow of the fireplace.

Right?

I peeked out again, and he'd walked around the front of the truck.

He turned to look in my direction again.

You know that feeling you get when someone keeps staring at you? Well, I think he kept getting it.

My heart stayed still, but it finally began beating once he turned to the woman and held out his hand, which she eagerly took.

I pursed my lips together in a private pout and watched him help her down the driveway, her bouncy ponytail bobbing and weaving as she made her way on the snow-piled drive. She looked at least thirty pounds lighter than me. I glanced down at my red and white pajamas. Okay, maybe more than that.

Did she come on the ferry in the middle of a snowstorm just for Nick?

Why did I care?

I found myself staring out the window at the flakes swirling around and piling up with such determination that I didn't realize Nick had crossed the street and was now pounding on my front door. I saw the side of him—arm raised—

smacking the door. My breath caught in the back of my throat.

I slowly slinked down the wall, squatting and pressing my body against the dusty drapes, praying he didn't see me. He knocked again, but this time, I saw a shadow fall across the floor as he pressed his forehead against the window to look inside.

Our eyes met, but I dropped my gaze quickly, pretending to search the carpet as if I'd dropped something into the weave.

"I see you in there," he said, laughing.

"I'm sure you do," I muttered.

"What was that?" he asked, still peering through the glass.

Damn single pane windows.

I stood up and unlocked the door.

Fiddling with my earlobe, I looked up at him.

"I was just looking for my earring I lost."

He grinned and glanced at my other ear.

"You might want to look for two earrings because you're not wearing any."

I pressed my lips together for a clever response, but I quickly gave up when he shoved a flashlight in my hand.

"I figured you needed this, seeing that you have no lights. Quite the storm." He bent down and picked up another flashlight and a radio from the stoop. "Since you like music, this operates on battery power." He shoved his hand into his puffy coat, which he was now wearing, and held a few batteries in his hand. "In case you run out in whatever device you decide to use this weekend."

I scowled at him and tried to hide my smile, but seeing the spark in his eyes made it nearly impossible.

"You like playing the part of the hero?" I joked.

"Is that how you see me?" His gaze turned a shade darker, and his eyes raked over my flannel pajamas as if he was imagining what was underneath.

My cheeks blushed.

"So far, you're the perfect neighbor," I promised him, dismissing the look in his eyes. I took the radio from him, and he propped the extra flashlight inside my door. "Thanks again. You should get back to your friend."

"Oh?" he asked, surprised.

I froze in embarrassment.

How was I supposed to know he brought someone back?

Oh, yeah. I wasn't, unless I was spying on him. I wanted to slap my palm against my forehead and slam the door he hung in his face, but instead, I did the adult thing and lied.

"I was just on my way to make sure I wasn't overfiring the stove when I saw you pull in with your guest." I bit my lip, waiting for a response.

"Is that so?"

"Yup."

"Well, thank you for being concerned about her wellbeing."

"Of course. Any friend of yours is a friend of mine." I forced down the thick amount of saliva that had accumulated in my throat and made me sound like a frog. "Are you sure you don't need one of these flashlights?" I pointed at the one he propped inside the door.

"Nah. I've got a generator."

"Seriously?"

He nodded. "I learned early on what's important to me. Electricity is one of those items."

"What are the others?" I asked, setting the radio on the carpet and standing back up to look at him.

The light flickering from the fireplace made him look insanely gorgeous, which was exactly not what I wanted to be reminded of. His thick lashes outlined his deep brown eyes as he watched me fidget.

To distract myself, I held out my hands, and he dumped the extra batteries in my cupped palms.

"I guess you'll find out in time." He winked, and it felt like I'd just walked off the teacup ride at Disneyland.

"Thank you." I took a step back and took in a deep breath. "For everything."

"Absolutely. If you need anything, you can call me or walk on over to the house."

"Even with . . ." I paused, unsure of what I was actually going to say.

"Yes. Even with one of my best friends visiting," he finished.

"Best friend?" I asked in disbelief.

"Why is that surprising?" He crossed his arms and looked thoroughly amused.

"Just with everything I've heard." I bit my lip.

"I mean, I haven't heard anything. I just asked around a bit. Well, I didn't ask. You happened to come up in conversation, and I learned you're not really into—" I stopped talking once I saw him shaking his head and laughing. "What?" I demanded.

"So you've been asking about me?"

"No." I cleared my throat. "I only wanted to make sure you aren't an axe murderer since you saw me in my bra and live across the street."

"That was the question you asked? Is Nick, my neighbor, an axe murderer?" He looked completely amused, which was somewhat infuriating.

"That's precisely what I asked."

"And?"

"It sounds like you have a lot of interests, but chopping people up isn't one of them." I cringed internally, wanting to sneak back into my Manhattan mode—sure of myself, dressed in a suit and heels, and ready to cut anyone down who dared look at me wrong.

Where did that girl go? Actually, I never liked that side of me, but she was handy to have on call.

"Good. I'm glad my secret's not out yet." He grinned wider and took in a deep breath, placing a sticky note with his number on top of the batteries I was still holding. "You know where to find me if you need me. Have a nice night, Holly."

"You too. Enjoy your best friend."

Enjoy your best friend?

I shut the door before he even had a chance to

turn around and quickly put the batteries on the floor so I could shut the curtains with one big heave.

The dust circulated into the air, and I let out a huge sneeze, followed by several more.

"Bless you, Holly."

"Thanks, Nick."

"Anytime." In between more sneezes, I heard his footsteps finally crunch onto the snow as he made his way down my driveway while I was left wondering if that really was his best friend.

Chapter Four

After eighteen long hours without power, the fun of camping by my stove had long since passed. When I woke up, Nick's truck wasn't in his driveway, and he never returned throughout the day. Not that I was standing and staring, but I happened to look when I was restocking the fireplace.

I organized my kitchen and emptied a couple of boxes that didn't involve repacking once the new floors came in. I still managed to feel super productive even though there wasn't any electricity. Maybe stacking bowls and plates wasn't rocket science, but it was nice to get something out of the way for the week, and it kept me from wondering about Nick.

My sister's power had come back on an hour ago, and she invited me over for dinner, which I happily agreed to. I hadn't showered since yesterday morning, and I desperately wanted to stand under warm water before changing into a new set of pajamas.

My phone beeped, and I glanced at the text from my sister.

Is it okay if my friend, Jewels, joins us? Her fiancé is out of town, and she wanted to drop off some books for me.

I typed back quickly.

Sure! As long as she doesn't mind that I'm only using you for your shower and will be dressed in pajamas.

My sister texted another response.

She won't even notice. Promise!

The fire in the stove had gone out, and I put the potato chips back in the kitchen, rolled my sleeping bag, and tossed my pillows on top. It wasn't hard to tidy up when there wasn't much stuff lying around.

I didn't really have a ton of possessions. It wasn't like I was trying to make a statement or anything, but I had a small space back in New York and most of my money went to rent and food. Whatever I had left, I managed to save for a rainy day. I just hadn't expected that rainy day to turn into a torrential downpour where I lost my job and all desire to continue working as an investment adviser.

But whatever. I was moving up and on with my bad self. Besides, my thrifty ways helped get me into this little charmer, and so far, living on the edge like this had been fun until the lights went out.

That being said, I liked to think I'd come home and the power would be on. I zipped my goose down coat over my pajamas, pulled on a red knit hat, and grabbed a bag with a new set of flannel pajamas inside. I was upgrading to a penguin print for the next round.

The snow had stopped several hours ago, but the temperatures were still frigid. It wasn't ideal to go out on the roads, but it was still light out, and I'd driven in the snow all the time in New York.

Well, not all the time, but a few times, and things worked out just fine.

Besides, I needed to see humans and I needed to shower, not necessarily in that order.

I glanced around my small living room before stepping outside and braving the cold weather on my way to my little Fiat. It looked even smaller sitting in a blanket of snow. I shoved the snow off the windshield and over my door so I could slide in without an avalanche. I glanced at Nick's driveway and noticed he must have left early because his tracks had been covered with the morning's snow.

I slipped in the driver's seat and started my little car's engine, hoping I'd be able to back right out of the driveway. As I slowly stepped on the accelerator, my car rolled backward, and I navigated onto the main road without issue. I saw two utility trucks down the road and excitement zipped through me at the thought of actually coming home to power.

There was a real chance!

As I made my way toward town and my sister's house, I gripped the steering wheel tightly and noticed how much it seemed like an eerie ghost town.

To get my mind off the deadness, I thought about all the things I wanted to do before my parents arrived for Thanksgiving. The floors would be a huge chore out of the way, and painting the paneling certainly helped, but it didn't exactly scream cute. I'd have to come up with some decorations that did, or my mother would sniff out uncertainty and make me wish I'd never left Manhattan.

I loved my parents. I really did, but my mother was high maintenance and my father didn't dampen that tendency. Growing up, there was never a spontaneous moment to be had. All events were documented, orchestrated, and properly celebrated. Whether it was a birthday party or a vacation, by the time it rolled around, the fun had been deflated because every detail had been planned to death.

No, thank you!

I'd much rather land in a city with no idea where I was headed or what I wanted to see until I stumbled upon it. Getting lost was always part of the adventure, part of life.

I slowed as I turned into my sister's driveway, the back of the car sliding slightly as I put my car in park and let out a deep breath.

I'd made it.

It didn't look like Jewels was here yet so maybe I could get in and out of the shower before she arrived. She was the town librarian. I'd only met her once when I first got here, but she was super sweet.

My sister opened the front door, and the beaming lights behind her beckoned me inside. I gave her a quick wave, grabbed my bag, and bounded out of my car toward her house. She had several pots of chrysanthemums that were now mounded with snow.

Winter had definitely arrived early.

Maddie gave me a quick squeeze and shut the door behind us. The smell of onion and garlic wafted through the home.

"What in the world are you making?" I asked, taking in a deep breath.

Her entry had a wine barrel that she'd turned into a table, with an autumn arrangement sitting on top, and a small bench next to it. All the walls were a soft yellow, and it screamed my sister.

She took my jacket from me and hung it in the closet.

"I'm making stuffed peppers."

"My favorite." I grinned and she nodded knowingly.

"I thought it was only fair since you moved all the way out here and had to suffer through your first power outage in the middle of nowhere."

"It wasn't that bad."

"You got supplies beforehand, right?"

I laughed and shook my head. "I tried. I really did, but the store was out of everything except chips, cookies, and crackers. Naturally, I stocked up."

"You've been sitting in the dark since yesterday?" My sister looked horrified. "How in the world are you tripping your way to the bathroom?"

"Nick dropped off a couple of flashlights for me last night." I tried to brush it off, but my sister was far too clever.

"Is that so?"

"Yup. I'm gonna go shower." I started up the stairs, but she grabbed my wrist and I turned around.

"Did—"

"Whatever you're going to ask, not even. He had company of the female variety waiting back at his house."

"Now that's the Nick I've heard about." She let go of my wrist and chuckled as I leaped up the final steps, suddenly feeling like I was back in high school with a nosy younger sister and absolutely no information to divulge.

I went into my sister's guest bath and turned on the shower, setting my bag on the counter. It felt amazing under the warm water, like all the dirt and grime from the horrid mustard carpet could just slide off and never return. I shivered at the thought and rinsed out the shampoo.

It was a shame Nick had a generator and wasn't even home to enjoy it. I would've stayed home the entire time just because I could. I shook my head and ran the conditioner through my hair as I heard the doorbell ring.

I quickly rinsed off and stepped out of the shower, dabbing and drying quickly, before stepping into my blue and white penguins. I got a few of my hair tangles out with my fingers and stuffed everything back in my bag, all while sliding my feet into my unicorn house slippers.

As I bounded down the steps to greet Jewels and my sister, I nearly toppled down the stairs when I heard his voice.

Nick was here.

I froze with one foot out in the open and the rest of me hidden behind the wall leading to the second floor. If he was in the entry, he'd see my foot, but if he'd managed to walk into the living room, I was in the clear. Regardless, I stayed motionless and prayed my unicorn wouldn't betray me.

"I didn't see her car in the drive and I didn't have her phone number. I gave her mine, but I didn't get hers. Anyway, I got worried something might have happened with the weather and all." His voice was gruff, but the tenderness behind it nearly melted me on the spot. "But I'm glad she's here. Will you just let her know that the power came back on about twenty minutes ago?"

"Will do, Nick," my sister told him. "That was really nice of you to come all this way."

"Well, she doesn't seem like the most well-prepared person, so. . ." His voice got louder with each word until he was standing in front of me. "I feel a certain obligation to make sure she makes it to the holidays for the sake of her family."

"I'm a perfectly capable human being," I huffed. "I survived just fine last night. In fact, I barely used the flashlight you brought over."

"What about the radio?" he asked, and I rolled my eyes, not wanting to give him an inch of forgiveness. "And I never said incapable, just not the most well-prepared."

"Hey, Nick," Jewels called up the stairs as the front door clicked shut.

I attempted to move past Nick, but his hand slid along my arm and my body hummed in response. I turned to playfully glare at him, but he was already letting me go and I wondered if I'd imagined it.

"Hi, Jewels. It's so nice to see you again," I told her, making my way down the rest of the steps.

"I didn't see you up there." She gave me a quick hug. "Is Nick staying for dinner?"

"I hadn't had a chance to ask him," Maddie responded, her eyes landing apologetically on mine.

"Actually, I've got some stuff I have to take care of back at the house or I'd love to," Nick said, his gaze moving along my body.

"A hot Tinder date?" Jewels teased, and Nick twisted his lips into a sexy pout.

"I'm more than that, you know." He smiled before adding, "But I gotta do what I gotta do." He sunk his teeth into his lips, and I nearly fell over thinking about his mouth elsewhere.

"Tinder?" My brow arched. "I wouldn't think you'd need a dating app."

"So I take it you don't swipe right?" He looked intrigued.

"I don't swipe up, down, left, or right." I looked over at Jewels and Maddie for guidance, but they were already making their way to the kitchen. "Too much work."

"That's the beauty of Tinder. There's no work required."

"I'm sure there are plenty of crazies and my finger would swipe right to them."

"It happens," he admitted. "But I've met a lot of interesting people, and it's been easy to avoid the ones who aren't looking for the same thing."

"Which is what?"

"I'm not looking for a serious relationship, so I just steer clear of anyone who is."

"So it's true what they say about you?" I asked.

"Who is *they* and what is being said?" He jogged down the last few steps, landing squarely in front of me. I ignored the charge that ran through me just from his moving closer.

"Nothing much. Just that you aren't exactly into relationships."

"That's true." He nodded.

"Is there a reason?" I asked, feeling my pulse rise as his gaze stayed fastened on mine.

"Many."

I took a step back and leaned against the front door. His eyes ran along my penguin pajamas, and a furious flutter in my belly made my body tingle with excitement for no apparent reason. I mean he was laying it out. Nick wasn't looking to date, and he enjoyed having absolutely no commitment. So why was I intrigued?

"On second thought, I think I will stay for dinner."

"Huh?" He brought me out of my daze.

"You heard me."

"What? Are you trying to get me on Tinder?"

"Never." He smiled and shook his head.

"And for the record, I didn't ask you to install my door. It was on my to-do list. And I didn't ask you to bring over flashlights or a radio. I would've been just fine without them. I'm fully capable and can handle a little snow and a power outage."

He shook his head. "I told you. I never said that you were incapable. Any woman who can tackle painting a room in the dead of winter in a bra with the door wide open is ... very capable."

I tilted my head and waited for more.

"Besides, I saw a unicorn peeking out at me from around the corner, and I knew it had to belong to the one and only Holly Wildes. I just wanted to tease you a little."

"Why would you want to do that?"

"Because you're cute."

"As cute as your best friend?" I moved away from the front door and felt his gaze on me as I walked toward the kitchen.

"Cuter," he said from behind. "Much, much cuter."

I stopped in the living room and waited for

Nick to catch up.

"You're difficult to figure out."

"I shouldn't be." He shook his head, smoothing his hand over his hair.

"Well, you are."

"Dinner is served," Maddie called from the kitchen.

"Saved by the bell," Nick muttered.

"You wish." I turned around and walked to the kitchen, where Maddie had spread the food out buffet-style on her kitchen counter.

We all dished up and sat around the kitchen table. Maddie had the curtains pulled wide open, and the sparkle of the snow was visible under her porch lights.

"I'm so excited about our guest speaker next week," Jewels began. "He's the leading authority on matchmaking and dating in the digital age."

"That sounds like fun." My sister nodded and glanced at Nick. I felt his gaze on me, but I wasn't sure why.

"Well, I don't think dating is any different than it was before Facebook or Twitter." I took a bite of the stuffed peppers. "I mean I can't imagine using a dating service or—"

"So you've never logged onto any kind of dating app?" Nick asked.

"No way." I shook my head.

"I'm tellin' ya. You're missing out not being on Tinder."

"Isn't that mainly for hooking up?" I asked. "Wait, never mind." I hid a smile, but Jewels' laughter filled my sister's tiny kitchen.

"Nick's favorite app is Tinder."

"Who'd you hear that from?" Nick asked, sitting up straighter.

"My sister, Natty."

My eyes widened in surprise. "You've dated Jewels's sister?"

Nick shook his head furiously. "No way."

"Oh, I see." I took another bite. "Dating is too strong of a word? She's just one of your best friends." I used air quotes and chuckled.

Nick laughed. "Actually, she is. She's also the town florist and engaged to her high school sweetheart, so unless I want to get my ass kicked to the moon and back, yeah. She's a best friend."

I was completely intrigued and confused.

"How many of these *best friends* do you have floating around town?" I asked.

Maddie looked at me, and then over at Nick, as if she had front row seats to Wimbledon.

"Well, there's Tori, Natty, and Sophie. Since Jewels moved back to Fireweed, she's making a strong case for a fourth."

"Aww, you shouldn't have," she joked.

"So which best friend did you have at the house last night?" I asked.

"Wouldn't you like to know?" He smiled and glanced over at Jewels, who seemed to be enjoying this for some odd reason.

"What can I say? I'm nosy."

He shook his head, laughing, and I knew I wasn't going to get my answer.

Chapter Five

"The floors look amazing," I told my sister. "It changes the entire feel of the cabin."

"I can't wait to see it. When will you let me come over?" My sister asked, wiping down the sink counter in the back room of the tea shop.

I measured a cup of peppermint leaves and sprinkled them into the stainless steel bowl where the rose petals and bits of licorice roots waited to be mixed. I tossed in a cup of lemon balm and blended the ingredients around in the bowl before transferring the tea into a tin.

"Give me a couple more days to make things better." I glanced over at her and she nodded. "I'm not sure what I'm going to do about the paneling I painted white though. Now that the wood floors are in, the walls look even worse."

"It'll all come together, but don't stress yourself out about Mom and Dad. It's impossible to please them."

I let out a deep breath, but it didn't make me feel better.

"I think if we each bought a home in their neighborhood, used Mom's decorator, and popped out two-point-five children, we'd start to make them happy," she said with a chuckle.

I shuddered at the thought. I'd grown up in Illinois in a perfect little village that called out to families of four, but it was impossible to meet anyone in a town of five thousand to create that perfect unit my parents craved for their two daughters. To say they were old-fashioned in their thinking would be an understatement. I didn't fault them for it, but I certainly didn't waste any energy trying to convince them otherwise.

"I know. I thought Mom was going to have a heart attack when she learned that not only was I leaving New York, but I wasn't coming home to Illinois."

"At least they're staying at my house," my sister chimed in.

"True, and thank you for that."

"Don't think I don't know why you bought a one-bedroom."

I followed my sister into the front of the tea shop and helped organize the newest additions to the shelves. With the holidays coming, we'd come up with a few pumpkin-laced teas and wintery concoctions, like gingerbread tea and peppermint mocha hot cocoa. I had no idea working in a tea shop would be so much fun.

The bell jingled, and I glanced toward the door to see a cute couple coming in from the cold. It had been several days since the snowstorm, but the temperatures had remained cold, keeping the white stuff on the ground.

"Back for the holidays?" My sister asked the woman, who nodded and glanced toward the man holding her tightly. It wasn't until he smiled that I recognized it was *the Anthony Hill*, lead singer of the Crimson Strings. I remembered hearing he had a place on the island, but I guess I never expected to actually see him wandering around town.

"We're here until mid-January." The woman glanced at me and smiled. Everything about her seemed warm and genuine. Her brown hair was piled in a braided bun with chunks falling around her face, and the gray leggings and bulky pink sweater looked like my type of clothing. "I'm Sophie, tea addict and town decorator."

My gaze flashed to my sister's and she grinned. So she'd known who Sophie was and hadn't said a word. Sophie was probably whom she'd gotten her info from about Nick's scandalous ways.

Suspicious.

"Nice to meet you. I'm Maddie's sister, Holly."

Without missing a beat, she wiggled out of Anthony's grasp and gave me a hug.

"So happy you decided to move to Fireweed. We just love it here and wish we could spend more time." She glanced at Anthony, and he was watching her like he'd just won the lottery. "If you ever need anything, let me know."

"You said you're an interior designer?" I asked.

She nodded and looked in her bag, pulling out a wallet and pinching a business card out of the leather.

"My store is at the north end of town."

"Thanks. I've got a mini fiasco with paneling I painted white and parents coming into town who are overly picky."

"I'd be more than happy to stop by," she offered.

"She would love that," Maddie said, looking at me. "Think of it as my housewarming gift."

"Really?" I asked in disbelief.

"Totally. Anything to avoid Mom and Dad's wrath tainting our Thanksgiving." My sister threw her head back and almost chortled before adding, "Don't get us wrong. We love our parents, but in small doses."

"I hear that," Anthony said, nodding. "All hands on deck if need be to avoid parental catastrophes near the holidays. Doesn't matter how old we get."

He walked over to one of the canisters and opened the lid.

"Smell this, babe." He motioned for Sophie, and she eagerly made her way over.

"That is the best ever. Who knew a tea called *Heartbreaker* would smell like vanilla and orange? This is a must," she said, holding onto the container.

Anthony was already sniffing another batch of tea when Sophie glanced at me. "So where did you move to?"

"I bought Frank's old cabin off State Road 26."

"*You're* Nick's neighbor?" Her brow arched and she glanced at my sister. "Why didn't you tell me?"

Maddie smiled but didn't answer as she motioned for Anthony to try our latest tea.

"What? What did I do?" I asked, placing my hand on my hip. "Has Nick said something bad about me? I've been trying to keep my music down ever since my eighties night. I didn't realize sound would carry so far, and I felt so bad for making him endure the endless loop."

Sophie's mouth curled up and she shook her head. "He hasn't said an unkind word about you. In fact, I think you've thrown him for a loop."

My brows furrowed and I shook my head. "I doubt that. Since he had dinner at Maddie's last weekend, he hasn't even so much as glanced in my direction when I'm pulling into my driveway. I was probably too hard on him about his Tinder account."

Anthony laughed and added another tin of tea to their collection for Maddie to measure out.

"He's a self-professed Tinder promoter, so he deserves anything you might have said." Anthony's smile from across the room was quite something. I could see why he was as popular as his music. He started talking to Maddie about how much tea they should get.

"That's true. If anything, it'll teach Nick to think before he speaks." Sophie nodded, and I was just confused. "Anyway, when would you like me to stop by? I'm pretty free over this next week."

"Could you two check it out now?" Maddie asked, measuring each of their teas into baggies. "I can hold the place down until closing, and I'll just feel better knowing your paneling debacle will be taken care of before Mom and Dad arrive."

I looked over at Sophie, who looked completely enthralled with the idea. "I'd love to."

"Are you sure? I don't want to interrupt your plans." I looked over at Anthony, who was shaking his head.

"Not at all. She'd do interiors 24/7 if she could," Anthony assured me.

Maddie rang them up while I untied my apron and hung it up in the backroom, feeling the excitement run through me at the thought of getting professional help.

"I'm just going to drop some books off at the library, and then we'll be right over," Sophie said as Anthony grabbed the paper bag full of tea.

"Sounds perfect. It'll be nice to get an opinion from someone who has vision. I'm severely lacking it at the moment. There are days when I wonder if I made a huge mistake," I confessed.

"From what I remember, Frank's place is brimming with possibilities." She winked, and Anthony draped his arm over her shoulders as they wandered out the door.

52

"See ya there," I called after them before turning my attention to my sister.

"What?" her voice went an octave higher than usual.

"So you're friends with one of Nick's best friends and you didn't say anything?" I asked.

"What's there to say?" she asked, her eyes twinkling with mischief. "I already warned you he had an active social life, which he validated over dinner."

I let out a sigh. "I suppose you're right, but there's just something about him. Half the time, I think I'm imagining a connection, and the other half, I think he feels it too."

"I wouldn't be surprised if he feels it, but the problem is that I think he feels it with a lot of females."

"I know, but maybe a fling is exactly what I need for the holidays." I wiggled my brows.

"Yeah, because that always works out well." She laughed and put the lids back on all the tea canisters.

"Truthfully, he's been giving me the cold shoulder all week, so it's all just a fantasy anyway." I grabbed my purse. "But I have been thinking about moving to Seattle and opening a Tinder account. Maybe that would make me more approachable."

"You have *not* been thinking about that." My sister crossed her eyes and stuck out her tongue.

"Really mature." I giggled. "Thank you for the gift of Sophie, by the way. Hope has been returned to my world of Holly Homemaker."

"Absolutely. Tell me what she thinks needs to be done, and I'll do whatever I can to help. I can paint, spackle, and tile. You name it and I'll help."

"Will do." I walked outside and felt the brisk air against my cheeks, and my mind wandered back to Nick.

It was obvious that my sister knew about his reputation, thanks to Sophie and whoever else around town, but I wondered what else she knew. I could tell my sister was keeping something from me. Was there never a time he dated someone from Fireweed?

I'd managed to daydream all the way home. As I was parking in front of my cabin, Anthony and Sophie pulled up behind. Sophie gave a quick wave, which I saw in my rearview mirror.

I opened my car door and climbed out. Sophie had already managed to drag Anthony with her to my car.

"This place is even cuter than I remembered. I love that door. Is that a new addition?" she asked, clapping her hands together.

"It is. I picked it out, and Nick actually hung it for me." Somehow, I felt she already knew all that.

"You have great taste," Sophie said, following behind as I walked up the steps to the door.

"Thanks. Besides the floors, that's about as far as I've gotten." I unlocked the door and pushed it open. Taking off my shoes, I put them on the jute rug. "You guys don't have to take yours off."

It was freezing, so I quickly made my way over to the fireplace and stocked it with wood and started the fire.

"Not a problem," Sophie said, already taking her boots off as Anthony did the same. "These floors are spectacular. Wow. We certainly don't want to be responsible for dinging them up."

"Thanks. I fell in love with the sample, but between the door and floors, I'm going to have to watch my pennies." I shut the door and glanced at Sophie's socks. I smiled at the brown turkeys adorning the yellow knit plaid covering her toes.

"I get excited about all holidays," she informed me.

"Well, you wear turkeys well."

"Thank you. I hadn't planned on pulling off my boots in public." She grinned. "So how do you want this space to feel?"

I took in a deep breath and pursed my lips together. "Cozy. I want it to feel cozy and well lived in. I love rustic mixed with quirky accents. I thought painting the walls white would give it a funky charm with all the wood contrasts, but it just looks drab. I'm not sure if I used the wrong paint or what. But I imagine a beautiful *Charlie Brown* Christmas tree over in that corner."

"I can see it now." She smiled. "Do you like the whitewash look?" Sophie asked, walking toward the wall where I wanted the Christmas tree.

"I love it, but I don't know how to do it."

Sophie ran her finger along the edge of the paneling that I painted and smashed her cheek against the wall, scanning the window for some reason.

"I think they actually put this paneling over

clapboard of some sort."

"Like the stuff that's on the exterior?" I asked, and she nodded.

"That would be pretty cool." I grinned.

"Do you mind if I step outside?" Anthony asked. "I'm getting a little hot."

I gasped and looked over at the stove. "Sorry. Totally. I forgot to turn down this little dial again. Nick warned me I'd burn the house down and I still forgot."

"No sweat." Anthony grinned. "Well, maybe a little, but I'll just be on the porch if you need me."

"You can keep the door open, and maybe it'll cool off."

Anthony nodded and walked outside.

I turned my attention back to Sophie.

"How do we know if it's clapboard?"

"I can carefully pry some of the paneling off in the corner to see what's behind."

I nodded excitedly. "That would be so awesome."

"Do you have a flathead or—"

I shook my head. "But I have a butter knife."

"That'll work."

I made my way to the kitchen, and Sophie followed the few steps it took.

"So Nick hung the door for you?" she asked, somewhat out of the blue.

I opened the silverware drawer and grabbed a knife.

"Yup. I think he felt bad about walking in on me half-naked and dancing to *What a Feeling*."

"Oh. My. God. I loved *Flashdance.* I watched it

a million times when I was a little girl."

"They just don't make inspirational movies like the eighties," I teased, only half-kidding.

Sophie chuckled and nodded in agreement, taking the knife from me.

"I happen to know that Nick doesn't usually feel bad about seeing half-naked women."

"I'm not sure if that's supposed to make me feel better or worse." I chuckled and so did Sophie.

"That came out wrong. I mean Nick usually just bounces from one life event to the next, rarely slowing down for much to register." She walked over to the corner and began sliding the knife under the paneling. "He just goes and goes and goes without giving much thought to . . ." She grimaced and bit her lip as she lifted the paneling away from the wall. "Bingo. We've got clapboard, and we could do a beautiful white wash over it to make it pop against the floors. What do you think?" Her brows shot up, bending the paneling just enough for me to get a peek.

"That's such great news." Now how did I get the conversation back to Nick? "Will it be costly?"

"It shouldn't be too bad." She handed me the knife. "Anyway, Nick's a really amazing friend, a good guy to have in your corner. He's the most loyal man in the universe, besides Anthony, and he'd move heaven and earth to make sure his friends were taken care of. Before my business took off, he helped me in little ways. He knew I was struggling to keep things afloat, and I'd get little envelopes with gift cards and cash tucked in the oddest of places. He'd always deny it, but I knew it was him."

"He seemed really sweet. Not that I'm a friend, but as a neighbor, he seemed genuinely helpful."

"Well, he usually saves that sweet side for his friends." She hid a smile. "And shows a different side to the others."

I tipped my head. "The others?"

"The ones we don't bother meeting most of the time." She smiled.

"Are there as many as my sister implied?"

"It's probably relative."

"Well, I'd imagine his looks only get him into trouble."

"Indeed." Sophie grinned.

"My impression of Nick is that he's a wannabe bad boy with a heart of gold. But he's definitely backed off since last weekend, so I guess I'll never really know," I teased, but I saw Sophie looking over my shoulder.

I froze, unwilling to turn around to see what or whom she was looking at.

"A bad boy with a heart of gold?" Nick's voice spun me right around and brought intense color straight to my cheeks.

Chapter Six

T he cabin had gotten eerily quiet.

"Only on a philosophical level," I assured him.

Nick's eyes brightened, and he looked even hotter than I remembered. His dark hair was shoved back from his face and his smile was even more addicting.

Anthony walked in behind Nick and glanced at Sophie.

"So what brings you by *this* time, Nick?" I asked.

"I saw that one of my best friends was parked in your driveway, and I thought I'd make my way over. Make sure you didn't burn the house down with Sophie in it or something."

"Or something." Sophie snickered, and I shot her a dirty look, but she only smiled wider.

"What?" Worry darted through Nick's eyes. "Did you almost burn the house down?"

"Not even."

Like I'd ever admit it.

I watched him open his arms to Sophie, and she walked over and gave him a big hug.

"So you come back to Fireweed and don't even tell Papa you're back?"

"Papa? Is he always this dramatic?" I asked Anthony.

"Always." He laughed.

"So anyway, before you so rudely interrupted, Sophie was explaining to me the possibilities of ripping out the paneling and white-washing the clapboard underneath."

"That's not what it sounded like you were talking about to me," Nick countered, a wicked grin spreading across his lips as he let go of Sophie.

"Is that so?" I asked, crossing my arms.

"Would you like a hug too?" he asked, making his way forward.

Yes!

"No. I'm just fine, thank you." I turned to look at Sophie. "So do you think this is something we can do before the holiday, or should we wait?"

She moved her lips into an exaggerated pout and thought about it for a few seconds before answering.

"Once we get the paneling down, it'll only take a few days to do the whitewash treatment," Sophie said, glancing at Nick. "The trick will be getting the paneling down and any noticeable

TEMPTING LOVE ON HOLLY LANE

holes filled without damaging your floors."

"Too bad I didn't know I had the best interior designer in the world on this island before the floors got replaced." I glanced at Nick, who looked down. My gaze followed to his boots, and he slowly walked backward to the rug, untied his boots, and slid them off.

"Planning on staying awhile?" I asked, and Anthony chuckled.

"I don't have anywhere else to be," Nick said, straightening back up.

"Slow night on Tinder, huh?" My brow arched.

His eyes connected with mine and a slow smile spread across his lips.

"And here I was going to offer to take down all the paneling for you. I guess I could fill up my time in other ways."

"I wouldn't put you through that." I glanced at Sophie, who seemed thoroughly entertained. "You've already done more than you should have by hanging the door."

He scratched his chin and smiled, looking over at Sophie.

"You know, I'm pretty handy too," Anthony spoke up from behind. "I bet Nick and I could hammer this out in a day."

This was unlike anything I'd ever experienced before. I had the world's hottest neighbor and the world's hottest rock star offering to dismantle my house for me. What was in the water here on Fireweed?

"I'd actually take them both up on this offer." Sophie piped up. "I can attest that Anthony is super capable with a hammer and crowbar."

"Seriously?" I asked.

"I'm a man of many talents." Anthony beamed.

Sophie walked over to him and slipped her arm around his waist.

"Not as many as me," Nick disputed.

"I can't let you guys do this. I was totally planning on hiring people," I told them both, but I could tell that for some reason their minds were already made up as they shook their heads. "Let me at least cook your dinners for a month or something."

"Sounds good to me," Anthony said, and Sophie shook her head.

"He can eat more than any man I've ever met. Careful."

"You don't owe me a thing," Nick answered, and I couldn't help but a feel a little wounded. "No dinners needed." He held up his hands, and I glanced over at Sophie, who looked conflicted.

"Well, when do you two masterminds think you can get this done?" Sophie questioned.

"I'm not busy tomorrow." Anthony looked over at Nick and waited for his response.

"Tomorrow works for me," Nick agreed.

"I honestly feel like I've landed in a magical place. I couldn't even get help when all my groceries exploded in the elevator of my apartment building back in New York, and now this?" I furrowed my brows. "I just . . . wow. Thank you."

"That happened?" Nick asked, and I nodded.

"No thanks needed. If you have time, feel free

to drop by my store this week, and we can look at some items you might like for here." She smiled and squeezed Anthony. "But we should get going to dinner and all."

"Well, thanks again." I gave Sophie a quick hug. "It's been amazing to meet you, and your generosity is just so—"

"Am I chopped liver over here?" Nick joked, and I couldn't help but fall for him a little more.

Sophie ignored Nick. "I'll see you at the shop, and welcome to Fireweed."

"I feel very welcomed." I gave a quick wave before they turned around and walked out of the house, leaving Nick and me alone.

"Have you heard a rumor about my cooking or something?" I asked him once they were out of earshot.

"What do you mean?" he asked, his brows pulling together.

"Well, every time I mention making you dinner, you reject my offer."

He laughed and shook his head. "I just don't want you to feel obligated to give me anything in return for being nice."

"Curious." I studied him.

"What's curious?"

"You are."

"How so?" he asked

"Well, you source out interactions with the opposite sex that are somewhat meaningless and easy to escape, yet you're the most generous neighbor I've ever come across."

"That's an interesting assessment."

I shrugged. "Just how I see it, but I have to tell you that turning down my offer to cook you dinner is starting to hurt my feelings."

"Is it?" he asked, his voice deepening.

"Possibly."

"How about tonight?"

"Dinner?"

He nodded.

"Well, I still have some canned chicken noodle."

"And so it begins." His laughter was low and stirred something deep inside me that was difficult to ignore.

"I'm kidding." I rolled my eyes. "But I have a question."

"What's that?"

"Have you been avoiding me all week?"

Surprise shot through his eyes. He shoved his hands in his back pockets, stretching out his chest. It was impossible not to notice the definition of his pecs under his shirt. The memories of a shirtless Nick hanging my door took over, and I suddenly felt my face warm as I waited for him to answer.

"Not on purpose. I actually didn't come over because of Sophie, but it was a handy excuse. Took the heat off temporarily."

"Why'd you think you needed an excuse?" My heart hammered in my chest. It wasn't like I thought he'd take me in his arms or anything, but there was something about him that drove me absolutely insane in a way I'd never experienced before. It was a mix of annoyance and obsession.

He was too cute for his own good, too cocky for my own good, and too oblivious about my feelings for it to matter.

"I don't know. It's never stopped me before." He sucked on his lip and my heart nearly fell to my toes.

"Now that doesn't surprise me."

"Actually, I wanted to see if you were free for dinner. I made lasagna and it's due to come out of the oven soon. It's a lot of food for one guy."

My jaw dropped to the floor. "Really? You cook?"

"I cook, clean, give great massages, and—"

"You had me at cook," I interrupted, not wanting him to go any further into his talents, especially since it didn't seem like I'd get to take part in any of them.

"So is that a yes for dinner tonight?" he asked.

"A definite yes if you promise to let me cook for you sometime."

"It's a deal." His eyes fell to my lips, and for a split second, I thought he might try to kiss me, but instead, he glanced at the fire and toward the door. "Well, how about in twenty minutes you make your way over?"

I squashed down the disappointment and nodded in agreement as he walked over to his boots and slid them on, not bothering to lace them up before he left. My mind drifted back to Sophie. Had I somehow stumbled into Nick's friend only zone, like being a neighbor automatically dropped me in a bucket that was impossible to climb out of?

I groaned at the thought, but I wasn't someone who was going to continue ogling over someone who wasn't into me. If those were the breaks, so be it.

I walked over to the fridge and took out a hard apple cider and flipped the top off. I'd give my feelings one more night, and if he didn't make an effort, I'd place him in the friend zone too. I took a sip of the spicy, cold cider and nodded my head, feeling more confident by the second.

Exactly.

Two could play this game. If all he wanted was a friendship with me, then fine. I took another sip and set my cider on the counter before moving toward the bedroom. A quick shower and change was only appropriate since I worked all day.

By the time I left my house, I'd managed to fit into my skinny jeans paired with a loose red sweater that was a bit low cut.

Okay, it was super low cut, and so was the camisole underneath it. I might as well make the best of my last attempt. I closed my front door and tried to shake away the butterflies. This wasn't a date, just dinner.

Between two neighbors. One of whom happened to be extremely sexy.

I had to admit, I was intrigued to see what his house looked like. I'd never actually seen anything more than what I assumed was a workshop. I made my way down the slippery steps, holding his two flashlights and radio to return.

Crunching down my driveway, I took in a deep

breath and tried to shake the ridiculous nerves that were running through me.

Nick was a nice guy who happened to be good-looking. I had no intention of moving from my new cabin, so maybe it was better if we kept things purely platonic. It would make the most sense.

I got to the end of the driveway and checked both ways before crossing the street to his long drive. The lights in his workshop were on, but he wasn't inside. I trudged down the drive, and my heart began thudding harder in my chest with each foot forward.

This was crazy.

It was only lasagna.

Nick's house came into view, and I was shocked at how beautiful it was. Three slate steps led to a large porch, which wrapped around the front and side of the log home. There were huge picture windows on each side of the front door.

Before I even reached the steps, Nick opened the door and smiled.

"Nice to have you, neighbor." He grinned, stepped outside, and reached for my hand. "The steps might be a little icy."

The moment his fingers wrapped around mine, I felt the connection again and looked up to see if he noticed it, but his expression remained unchanged.

"Thanks for inviting me over."

"Pleasure's mine." He let go of my hand the second I was on safe ground, and my heart dipped.

"Such a beautiful home. I didn't know it was a log home. You can't really see it from the road."

"Thanks. It's been a labor of love."

Once I stepped inside, I knew exactly what he was talking about. Every beam, post, and beautifully carved banister created a welcoming foyer. The same slate from outside had been carried into the entry, and an open second-story looked down from above.

To my left was a living room and to the right, a dining room. I could smell the garlic and basil from the lasagna wafting through the air. Kissing definitely wasn't on the menu.

"Smells delicious." I glanced at Nick, who gave a quick nod.

"Thanks. It's just setting up. I can give you a tour, if you'd like." He smiled, reaching for my hand again.

"I'd like that."

"So down this hall are the kitchen and the great room with a pretty mammoth hearth. It's kind of the centerpiece of the house. I wanted to make sure I could see it from the kitchen and the dining room."

The house looked modest from out front, but it was really spacious inside. The great room was two stories high. I looked up and saw more of the exposed beams and a balcony overlooking the great room.

"Upstairs are bedrooms and a bonus room."

"The furniture is so gorgeous," I said, admiring the sectional that had an ornately carved wood frame and a beige fabric covering overstuffed cushions.

"Thanks. I've really enjoyed getting to make all the pieces."

"You made all these?" I asked, scanning the stools dotted along the granite breakfast bar, another smaller dining table in the center of an eating nook, and a large, blocky, rustic coffee table.

"Yup. It's what I was born to do."

I saw a glint of pride surface behind Nick's gaze, and I could see he loved what he did.

"I can see that." I nodded, admiring the space.

"Would you like to see upstairs?"

"Sure. It's probably the only time I'll see it, so why not?" I grinned, and he parted his lips but shut them quickly without saying a word.

"What?" My brow arched.

"Nothing. There's another staircase over here. It's not as fancy as the one out front, but it does the job."

He opened a door next to the kitchen and turned on a light. It felt like a secret corridor as I scaled the steps after him.

"This is the only part of the house that has drywall, and I'm looking forward to getting rid of it, but I just haven't had the time."

"Well, you've obviously been busy."

We reached the top, and I spotted the balcony overlooking the foyer, but to my immediate right was a short hallway.

"This is the owner's suite."

"I take it that's you?" I grinned.

I couldn't have picked out a better room for Nick if I tried. The king-size bed was rustic and masculine, but the gray duvet and matching pillows piled on the bed threw me.

"I didn't take you as a duvet kind of guy." I walked into his bedroom and he quickly followed, chuckling.

I glanced out one of the windows that pointed toward the front of the house. There was a distant glow between the branches of thick conifers.

"Is that my little cabin?" I asked, craning my neck to see better.

"It is." He smiled.

"Were you spying on me?" I teased, knowing I'd be nothing more than a tiny dot.

"Absolutely."

I followed him out of the bedroom and across the balcony, where I could see into the foyer on one side and the great room on the other, until we hit another hall with the remaining bedrooms.

There was something off about Nick since I'd arrived. The carefree Nick that I'd gotten used to seemed to have disappeared, replaced with a quiet version. By the time we walked down the stairs into the foyer, it was driving me nuts.

"Is everything okay?" I asked, looking into his brown eyes. "You seem a little more uptight than at my house."

His lip quirked up slightly and he shook his head.

"Sorry. I'm just . . ." He stopped himself.

"What? Do you need me to go back home? I can. It's totally fine if Tinder is calling."

Nick's low, gravelly hum of a laugh echoed into the foyer, and I got a tingle from my head to my toes.

"So what's up with not dating people on the island?" I asked.

His eyes widened.

"You've seen how small of a place it is. Can you imagine how well that would work come break-up time?" He cocked his head toward the kitchen and I nodded, following right behind.

"So you're assuming any relationship you have would go down in a blaze of glory?" I questioned.

"It's a known fact." He pulled a knife out of a wooden block and began cutting into the lasagna. It looked amazing, and so did the garlic bread sitting next to it. "Relationships and me are like a pickle and peanut butter sandwich."

I smacked the counter and he jumped.

"Have you actually had pickles and peanut butter?"

He stopped cutting and looked at me oddly. "No. Have you?"

"Yeah. I have, and it's surprisingly good. It was a dare in college."

"If you think that's a good combo, you might not like the lasagna. It's pretty basic."

"All I'm saying is that you shouldn't shut yourself off from the possibilities. You might like pickles and peanut butter."

"Possibilities from what in particular, Holly?"

The way he said my name made me want to stand in front of him and do jumping jacks and point at myself.

"See? You don't even know what the possibilities are. Talk about missing out in life." I took a piece of garlic bread and sat in the chair, pretending not to sulk about my permanent friend status as he poured us each a glass of wine.

Chapter Seven

"Is that a hot tub?" I asked, taking the last bite of the most amazing lasagna in the history of noodles. I was pointed toward the back window, and all through dinner, I'd tried to figure out what I was looking at on the patio.

"It is." He sat back in the chair.

"My boyfriend in high school always tried to get me into his. Well, there were a lot of things he tried to get me to do." I glanced at Nick and he was smiling.

"He wasn't able to convince you?" Nick asked.

"Nope."

"Poor guy. Well, I guess I shouldn't even bother then." He wiped his mouth with a napkin, and I forced my eyes from lingering on his lips. Men weren't supposed to have such luscious lips.

Maybe the second or third glass of wine was getting to me. Maybe he had average lips and the alcohol made them look bigger.

"It's freezing outside," I told him.

"That's what makes it so relaxing. You just sink into the steaming water and let your worries drift away. It's even better when it's snowing."

"Sounds nice." And it did.

"It *is* nice." He stood up. "Ready for some limoncello sorbet?"

"That sounds even better." I took my plate and the almost empty bowl of garlic bread over to the counter and watched him move through his kitchen, opening the freezer.

"How about if I try a pickle and peanut butter sandwich, you'll go into the hot tub with me?" He spun around holding the sorbet.

"Now?" I chirped.

"Or whenever. It doesn't have to be tonight." He licked his lips and his eyes fell to mine.

"I don't have a suit," I muttered. "Not that it matters, I guess. You've seen me in the equivalent of a bikini top."

"True." He nodded, lifting his gaze.

"Is this a dare?"

"Would it help or hurt the cause?" He asked, his brows furrowing together.

"I rarely turn down a dare."

"Then it's a dare." He smirked.

"From one neighbor to another?" My brow arched.

"A dare from one friend to another."

Friend.

I narrowed my eyes at him before glancing toward the hot tub.

"Can we eat the limoncello in the hot tub?" I asked.

He dropped one of the bowls on the counter and scrambled to catch it before it hit the floor.

"I don't see why not."

Now or never.

"Then, I'll meet you out back." I didn't bother to look at Nick as I made my way to the sliding glass door, but I felt his eyes on me every step of the way.

Afraid I was going to talk myself out of it, I unlocked the door, walked out onto the concrete patio, and removed the hot tub cover. The fresh smell of chlorine mixed with the chill in the air was odd, but somewhat exhilarating, especially as the water hissed and snapped with bubbles. I glanced through the window and saw Nick in the kitchen, scooping the sorbet and looking like this kind of thing happened every day of the week.

I suppose for him, maybe it did.

I looked behind me and beyond the patio. Looked like nothing but forest.

I could do this.

I took in a deep breath and slid down my skinny jeans, which were already too tight from dinner, and quickly pulled my sweater and camisole up and over my head. I draped everything over the hot tub cover and climbed up the steps, dipping my toe in first.

The water wasn't quite scalding, but it was

really hot. I glanced into the house again, and he was turning around so I slid into the water before he could see me.

The heat wrapped around most of my body as my neck stuck out of the water.

"I wasn't sure you were actually going to do it," Nick said, coming onto the patio.

"I'm a woman of my word."

I noticed he tucked a new bottle of wine under his arm as he handed me my bowl of sorbet.

"Champagne," he said after seeing me eye the bottle.

He set it on a patio chair and walked back into the house, where he grabbed a couple of flutes.

I took a bite of the sorbet and closed my eyes from delight. It was like I was experiencing sensory overload. Between the sweet and tart of the sorbet, the chill in the air, the heat under the water, and Nick, I could barely keep my head on straight.

"This. Is. Amazing." I opened my eyes to see Nick tugging his sweater over his head, and my breath caught.

It shouldn't have. I knew this was the process. He wasn't going to get in with a sweater and jeans, but I wasn't really thinking this through.

"You okay?" he asked, tilting his head.

"Totally. I've just never had sorbet this good." I smiled and took another bite, watching him bend over, presumably to take his jeans off.

Neighbors. Friends. Whatever this was, it made my night interesting.

Before climbing in, he popped the cork on the

champagne and poured us each a glass. He set them in the cup holders and balanced his bowl next to them.

He didn't bother with the steps. Instead, he hoisted himself up with his arms, and his body moved like a male gymnast as his legs came over the top and he slid into the tub with barely a wave in my direction.

It was the sexiest thing I'd ever seen. It didn't hurt that he was wearing black boxers.

"You okay over there?"

"Doing just fine, friend." I grinned and took a sip of my champagne.

"Don't chug it. The bubbles can really get to a person in a hot tub."

"Do you tell all the women that?" I giggled and his expression fell slightly.

"Actually, you're the first."

"The first you told that to or the first to climb in the hot tub?"

His smile returned and he looked up toward the sky.

"You're the first *anyone* to be in this thing besides me."

"Really?" I asked, completely not expecting to hear that.

He nodded and took a bite of the sorbet.

"It's just kind of my place to relax." He watched me carefully, and even though I was ninety percent underwater, a wave of goosebumps ran across my skin.

"Well, by the looks of it, you need a place to relax. You work your fingers to the bone." I took a gulp of champagne instead of a sip. "Besides making your home a home, designing and building all the furniture inside it, and running a company, you have to devote hours upon hours chugging away back and forth on the ferry, keeping your Tinder profile up-to-date. It's gotta be exhausting."

He laughed and put his empty bowl on the ledge.

"Life can be very exhausting," he agreed.

He was a few feet away from me, sitting on one of the hot tub's reclining benches. It would be so easy to float over to him, but he looked at ease and like he was truly enjoying being out here with his neighbor-turned-friend.

I just couldn't ruin his night like that.

"You're a fun girl." His eyes connected with mine and a shiver shot down my spine. There was something about the way he was looking at me that made me wonder if maybe I should float in his direction.

"I have my moments." I smiled, propping my bowl in his before leaning back in the water.

"Something tells me you're full of them." He stretched his arms along the edge of the hot tub.

I shook my head. "Only since I moved here. Fireweed is freeing. I don't have angry bosses, disgruntled clients, or an apartment that smells like whatever my neighbor is cooking. Plus, I have a job that is fun. What more can I ask for?"

Nick's smile widened. "What more could you ask for?" He nodded. "Exactly. Life is pretty good."

"It is." I sank back and rested my head against some sort of pillow contraption.

"What brought you out here?" he asked as the Jacuzzi bubbles popped around my ears.

"I got let go from my job as an investment adviser. I'd been there for seven years, so my severance package was pretty decent. My sister talked nonstop about Fireweed, and when I visited, I fell in love. I used my entire severance package on Frank's place and haven't looked back since."

"Wow. I'm impressed."

Nick's knee knocked into mine, and I immediately felt like I was back in tenth grade again, where every touch and connection was jolting.

"It's been a wild ride so far. My parents are coming out to visit us at Thanksgiving. They're a bit judgy." I laughed.

"You sound nervous."

"They make me that way. Always have and always will. My sister and I didn't exactly follow their plans for us."

"Which were what?" he asked, genuinely interested.

"Go to college, get married, pop out some kids, live down their cul-de-sac, and let them babysit their grandchildren." I smiled.

"My sister and I got to the first step, but after that, my parents' plan blew up. It will make Thanksgiving extra fun this year since I lost my job, am still single, and have a house in disarray. I'd hoped to at least have Christmas lights up or something to make it look like I have life under control."

Nick laughed and moved his arms over the water, creating a gentle ripple.

"Christmas lights always make things better." He grinned. "But I hear that. I was supposed to go to law school, or at the very least, enter some graduate program, but four years was more than enough for me."

"I promise I won't bring up Tinder after this, or at least not for the rest of the night, but I'm curious why you live on Fireweed if your entertainment is mostly centered across the water?"

"I love the people here. I love the lifestyle. The other . . ." He shrugs. "I don't know. It's just for fun, and regardless of what your sources think, I'm really not all *that* successful."

"Well, recently, you've been one of my main sources." I giggled.

He laughed and nodded. "Exactly my point."

A few minutes of silence sat between us, but it wasn't awkward. It was just peaceful. My mind had stopped spinning about my parents coming out and all the house stuff I had left to do, and things felt blissful.

"So what else did the high school boyfriend not get his way with?"

"Wouldn't you like to know?" I asked, trying to feed him some of his own medicine.

"I really, *really* would." Nick floated closer to me, and I took the last sip of my champagne. "Would you like some more?"

"I wouldn't want you to have to get out."

"I can reach it from here," he assured me.

Before I had a chance to answer, he stood up, reached over the hot tub toward the bottle on the table, and snagged it. His body was dripping wet as he poured us each a glass and then repeated the process to put the bottle back on the table. He looked delicious and perfectly in reach, considering all the alcohol I'd downed.

I dropped my gaze quickly toward the bubbling water before he spun back around.

"So you ripped out your high school boyfriend's heart and—"

"Not even," I protested. "He was a total creep. I caught him cheating with his sister's best friend during one of her sleepovers. It was the biggest high school scandal to hit that town in years."

"Must have been a small town."

"Painfully small. After that, I decided I'd wait to find the love of my life in college."

"How'd that work out?" he asked.

"Not well." I laughed. The champagne was definitely getting the better of me, and I was happy for it. "I went with the same guy for the first two years of college, but when that ended eerily similar to what happened with my first boyfriend, I boycotted relationships."

"Permanently?" He looked concerned as he took a sip of his champagne.

"Oh, I still had fun." I grinned. "Well, you've seen the neck massager."

Nick nearly spit out his drink as I laughed wickedly.

"Kidding." I pushed water in his direction, and he stood up to avoid a wave to the face. "I just stopped being so worried about relationships and enjoyed the fun of dating and meeting new people."

"How long did that last?" he asked.

"Who said it's over? Who knows? Maybe I'll join Tinder."

"It's not as fun as it's cracked up to be."

"How so?"

He floated a little closer to me. "On the rare occasions you get to know someone, you find out they're as jaded as you are."

"So you're jaded?" I asked, surprised to hear him admit it.

"Extremely so."

It took everything I had not to float the rest of the way to him and wrap my legs around his waist, but he was my neighbor, who turned out to be a really good listener, and I suddenly didn't want to spoil the combo.

"How come?"

"You know how you bounced back pretty easily?" he questioned. "First high school and then college?"

"It wasn't particularly easy, but I wasn't going to let a couple of buffoons ruin my fun forever."

"Well, I didn't bounce back quite so easily."

"You were cheated on?"

He nodded. "Yeah. I thought I was going to marry her. We were best friends all through junior high. We started dating in high school, and it even lasted into college . . . until Brock."

"Brock?" I laughed. "What kind of name is Brock? Was he a football player?"

"How'd you guess?" A spark flashed through Nick's eyes. "Anyway, at the same time that happened, my parents, who had been married for twenty years, got a divorce, and voila. I decided that whole thing just wasn't for me."

"So you compartmentalize all relationships," I said, more for my benefit than his. "That's why you have friends, neighbors, and Tinder."

"I suppose you could say that. Frank was a hard one to categorize though." Nick's smile was infectious and made me want so much more.

"So I'm clearly in the friend zone for no fault of my own but location. Had I set up a Tinder account and moved into a small apartment in Seattle, my luck might be different?" I teased.

"I would say you've got pretty good luck in not having that as an option."

I scowled and took another sip of champagne. "But the problem is that I'm a woman who likes choices. Frank might have been okay with it, but I don't like to be categorized or compartmentalized or . . ."

"Put in a box?" he asked, standing up.

"Exactly. Don't you want to live a limitless life?" I asked, feeling rather impassioned about the subject. "You don't seem like a rigid guy until you get to this topic. Then you turn into Mr. Freeze, and nice women, like myself, get put in the neighbor bucket with no way out." I waved my hands at him. "Not that you haven't been an amazing neighbor to have."

He looked down at me while I stayed sitting in the hot tub, my mind looping with mostly nonsense thanks to the wine and champagne. I wanted to say more, but I kept my mouth shut because it wouldn't matter anyway. Once we hit the age of thirty, we were all set in our ways, and we'd both hopped, skipped, and jumped past that number.

"Holly, I didn't mean to put you in a bucket or make you feel like I did. You're so much fun. Your energy is off the chains, and I can see myself hanging out with you because you're just so fun . . . so different than who I usually meet."

"Isn't that kind of your fault? I mean, you set up your profile. You're the only one who can slide right on that app and set your preferences."

He ran his tongue across his lips, and I was certain he was about to kiss me. The energy between us nearly crackled, yet I was frozen with fear. Would I really be able to pull off a fun fling for the holidays?

His eyes darkened as he brought his hand through the water and reached out for me. He sank into the water as his hand rested on my shoulder.

My breath caught in the back of my throat as I moved off the bench and floated toward him. With disoriented reasoning, I looped my arm around his neck and brought myself in to him.

Nick let out a low growl as he rested his forehead against mine.

"I really like you, Holly. I don't want our relationship to change."

"It won't," I whispered as his hands ran along my back.

My heart was pounding a million miles a minute as his eyes stayed on mine. Feeling him this close to me made my entire body vibrate with excitement.

I closed my eyes, feeling his thumb trace my bottom lip, and a wave of shivers ran through me as his lips slowly replaced his thumb. My mouth parted slowly as I beckoned his tongue, inviting him for more.

He buried his fingers deep into my hair as he kissed me harder, and I let out a quiet moan.

Sprinkles turned to showers, and I knew a kiss was all I was going to get. He'd already been looking for a way out, and nature provided it.

Chapter Eight

"You did not," Maddie said, shaking her head. "I don't believe it for a second."

"I totally did. He dared me to at some point get in his hot tub if he agreed to eat a pickle and peanut butter sandwich."

Maddie's lip curled in disgust before quickly grinning.

"Come to think of it, he never did eat the sandwich." My brows shot up.

"I can't believe that after everything you know about him, you'd let yourself kiss him." She wiggled her brows. "That's one step away from the deed."

"First of all, it was only a kiss."

"In your bra and underwear, in the middle of winter, soaking in a hot tub." She hid a smile.

"Technically, it's still fall." I grinned. "Besides,

it was harmless fun."

"But he's allergic to commitment."

"How do you know I'm not? I've had my fair share of fun nights in Manhattan that had no strings attached."

"With Leo from accounting?" My sister laughed.

"Hardee-har-har." I rolled my eyes. "The occasions might have been few and far between, but they do exist and didn't involve anyone from accounting, marketing, or sales. Anyway, it's completely innocent fun, and besides, he's already broken one of his own rules. I live on Fireweed."

"Which makes the whole thing strange." Maddie eyed me. "And like you're trying to read something into this more than a fling."

I looked out the window of the tea shop, and the sidewalks were flooded. I swore it hadn't stopped raining since the hot tub last night.

"Truthfully, I don't expect it to get very far, but I'm going to have fun with my hot neighbor for as long as it lasts. Or at least until someone else catches his attention with a more appropriate zip code."

"Let's say he had a date tonight with someone in Seattle." She folded her arms. "How would you feel about that?"

My stomach tensed.

"Well, considering we only kissed, I can't exactly expect him to only have eyes for me. That wouldn't be very realistic."

"You didn't answer my question. How would

you feel?" She peeled off a sticker and slapped it on a tin.

"A dart of jealously might splinter my soul momentarily." I pressed my lips together and thought about it for a second longer. "But I'd get over it."

"Sure you would."

"Eventually. It might take forty-eight hours or so." I laughed. "You know what the issue is?"

"What?"

"He's just so damn sexy. I don't want to miss an opportunity." I sighed. "Even if it was only a one-time thing, I think I'd actually be content. I'd rather have him once than not at all."

"Really?" My sister looked surprised.

"Yup."

"Not sure I believe it."

"I'm not sure I do either, but I'm willing to give it a go. Doesn't matter because I'm getting way ahead of myself considering we shared an innocent kiss and nothing more."

"Then why are you blushing?"

The UPS man walked up the sidewalk, carrying a box, and I'd never been so happy to see him. This conversation was going nowhere.

"While I'm slaving away at the shop, do you realize I have two really good-looking men tearing out paneling at my house?" I turned the music up, which happened to be Dolly Parton's *9 to 5*. I eyed my sister.

"I'm surprised you didn't use a sick day." She grinned.

"I didn't know I had any." I opened the door.

"Hey, Danny."

"Hi, Holly. Just one today. Smells like lavender." He sniffed the box and I hid a chuckle.

"Sorry. That can really seep into clothing," Maddie said, walking around the counter.

"No problem. I'd rather have that smell than most." He set it on the counter and scanned it.

"Would you like your usual?" Maddie asked, grabbing a paper cup.

"Definitely need the caffeine today. Even though we live in the rainy state, everyone seems to forget how to drive during these storms."

"And it's only going to get worse with the holidays." Maddie shook her head, pouring the boiling water over the tea bags.

Danny pretended to shiver. "Don't remind me. I'm just glad I have this route."

Maddie handed Danny the cup while I opened the box. We'd been waiting for this delivery from Hound Island from our favorite lavender farm. My sister met the owner at our farmer's market over the summer, and she'd invited us both to her farm, but neither of us had made it over yet. Every time I brought it up, Maddie would turn red and come up with an excuse not to go.

"Thanks for the tea, Maddie," Danny told her. "You two always have the oddest assortment of music."

Dolly's song changed to INXS and I nodded in agreement.

"What can I say? We're eighties girls," I warned. "You can't expect too much from us."

"Is that what it is?" He winked at my sister

and walked his way out of the store.

"I think he has a crush on you," I teased. "Well, he's cute and he's got good legs."

"Why do you suppose he always wears shorts, even in the winter?" My sister asked, sliding onto a stool.

"Maybe it's how he impresses the ladies."

My sister laughed.

"So Mom and Dad are renting a car. They don't want to bother us for a trip to and from the airport."

"Which is code that they want their own transportation in case of an emergency, like there are bed bugs in your sheets or something." I grinned. "It's nice of them, whatever the reason."

"They'll be getting in on Tuesday."

"Tuesday? I thought they were coming on Wednesday. That only gives me four days to make the house presentable."

"I know."

"When are they leaving?"

"That Sunday."

My shoulders sank.

"That's a long trip."

"It'll be fun," she assured me, but it looked like she was trying to assure herself instead.

"I know. I just hope we don't have to endure day after day discussing all the ins and outs about how we're single. Do you think we could rent someone from Tinder to carve the turkey so it looks like one of us has a boyfriend?"

My sister laughed. "I don't think that's how it

works."

"I'll check with Nick just in case."

My sister flashed a knowing grin.

"What's that about?" My brow arched.

"He's already sneaking into casual conversation."

"Only because it was *casual*." I shook my head. "He's a friend."

My phone buzzed and I glanced at the message.

Anthony said they're close to finishing the main areas. Do you want them to do the same in the bedroom?

"What's up?" my sister asked.

"I guess they're already done with most of the main living section. Sophie asked if I wanted them to continue into the bedroom."

"I'd say so." My sister nodded.

"Are people always this nice around here?"

"For the most part. There are a few cranks here and there, but they tend to keep to themselves."

"Have you ever been to Nick's house?" I asked.

"More casual conversation?" My sister shook her head. "Not inside. I dropped off Sophie once, but I just pulled in the driveway. It looked really cool from what I could see."

"Yeah. It's pretty sweet." I walked over to the laptop and continued entering our inventory.

"So have you given any more thought to becoming a partner?" my sister asked.

"I wasn't sure you were serious." Maddie had mentioned the idea when I was still packing in New York, but I didn't know if she was serious because she hadn't brought it up since.

"Definitely serious. Right now, we're only open five days a week, but if you came onboard as a partner, I wouldn't have to pay you a salary and we could be open seven days a week."

I chuckled.

"Kidding. We'd split the profits fifty-fifty. By my figures, by being open two more days a week, we'd be doing ourselves a huge favor."

My sister's blue eyes were filled with excitement, and I certainly didn't want to disappoint her. I knew her shop was doing well, and I was grateful to be working here while I got my head on straight, but this was her dream. Now that I had a little bit of time, I kind of liked the idea of figuring out what my dream might be.

"You don't have to figure it out right away." My sister waved her hands at me.

"It's a really generous offer. I'm just still in that zone of not knowing what I really want to do with the rest of my life."

"Just know the offer is always there."

"Thanks. I appreciate it. The idea is really appealing, but I want us to both think about the pros and cons."

"The finance major is at it again." My sister shuddered.

"With a minor in ancient history," I reminded her.

"Right, because those two always go

together."

"In a perfect world, they do."

A huge group wandered into the shop, and I made my way behind the counter. A few of the women broke from the group and began sniffing teas while the others wandered over to order some fresh brewed. The guys lingered near the door until they realized they could order drinks. I counted the number of guys and number of girls and realized some of the women were single or polygamous. It was nice to see a mix like that. In New York, it always felt like the marrieds went out and the singles went out.

Maddie took their orders and I made their teas. My sister and I made a good team. There was no doubt about it.

The women who were sniffing the teas brought the tins they chose over and set them on the counter, ordering two ounces of each. Two were brunettes and one was a blonde. The blonde had an edgier look, with choppy bangs and a bob.

"Are you in town for the upcoming holiday?" My sister asked the group.

"We are. We rented a cute little house on the shore for eight of us," one of the brunettes said.

"That's cool," I responded as I scooped the loose tea for their orders.

"It doesn't matter what time of year it is here. It's always so cozy," my sister added.

"Yeah. Andrea used to date someone who lived here, and she's been hooked ever since."

My gaze darted to the brunette, and I followed

hers to the blonde who was smiling.

"You never know. Maybe I'll run into him," Andrea said, grinning wickedly, and my stomach tensed.

"Is that why you made us come here and not Leavenworth for the holiday?" Her friend jabbed her. I looked down at the piles of tea and hurriedly finished up their orders. "Ever since you two broke up, you've never stopped comparing everyone you slept with to him."

The odds were slim to none that she dated Nick. Nick didn't date, first of all. He only hooked up, and this sounded like a relationship. I placed the stickers on each of the baggies as my sister rang them all up. I kept pushing down the weird feeling that wanted to sprout up.

It didn't matter anyway.

"Well, you keep your eyes out for your Nicky-poo, and I'll be on the prowl for the rock star when we're buying our turkey." The brunette nearly cackled, and the hairs on the back of my neck stood up.

"The rock star is married." I looked up at Andrea's friend and stared at her.

Sophie was such a sweetheart, and it killed me hearing these women talk like this. Did she have to put up with this crap all the time? Anthony only had eyes for Sophie. I could tell by the way he looked at her, touched her, joked with her. It was the kind of love I hoped I'd someday get, but until then, I was going to do my best to stomp on these groupies.

"That wouldn't stop me." The brunette giggled

and glanced at Andrea, who nodded in agreement.

"Me neither." Andrea took her bag of tea from my sister, who suddenly didn't want to let go of the sack.

"Well, from what I heard, he's in California until after Christmas," I informed them. My sister turned around and held in a snicker.

"Isn't that our luck?" the brunette huffed.

"Well, that's why I always set my sights lower. I doubt Nick is anywhere but his house. All he ever did was work." She smiled almost giddily, and I pushed down the very bit of jealousy I told my sister I'd be able to handle.

"Have fun on Fireweed," I said, handing Andrea her bag.

"Oh, I intend to." She winked and walked out the door with the rest of the group.

"Ugh." I sank onto the stool. "Poor Sophie."

"I was going to say the same about you." My sister squeezed my shoulder. "You okay?"

"Yeah. I mean . . . I thought he didn't really date, and *Andrea* made it sound like they were in a relationship."

"Maybe it was a non-relationship that was long-term," my sister offered.

"I'm sure that's it. But it doesn't matter. I know nothing is going to come of this whole thing."

"You don't know that." She grabbed the tins and took them back over to the shelves. "Don't let those groupies get you down."

I laughed. "Not even in the slightest. Should I

warn Nick?"

"I wouldn't touch the topic with a ten-foot pole." My sister shuddered. "Literally. No matter how you start the conversation, it'll come out sounding bad. Like either you're the crazy one or jealous or nosy. The list is endless."

"Great. And I'm all of the above." I chuckled, feeling tension in my entire body. It was like I had a sudden urge to get to Nick before the blonde bobblehead jumped out in front of him.

"Did you notice she looked kind of like a bobblehead?" my sister asked.

"I totally noticed." I could always depend on my sister to lift me up at the expense of others, but she'd always put me right in my place at the same time.

"A good reason to be grateful for these manly shoulders we have. Our heads always look firmly in place." Maddie bobbed her head to the side and I groaned.

"At least we don't need shoulder pads." I glanced at the clock and noticed the shop was supposed to close ten minutes ago. It was nice to have a job where I wasn't on pins and needles waiting for the second hand to tick by.

That being said, I was really excited to go home to see the progress on my cabin.

And possibly one of the men who was making it happen.

"Do you want to come with me to the house?" I asked my sister.

"I thought you wanted to wait?" Her brows rose.

"Nah. I'm dying to see what it looks like without the paneling."

"Paneling has its place," Maddie informed me.

"Yes, it does, but I just didn't see it for the look I was going for. I plan on growing old in this cabin, so I might as well make it how I want."

Maddie untied her apron and went to the back room while I saved what I was working on in the computer.

It was already dark outside, but that didn't matter. Everything I was looking forward to seeing was on the inside.

"I think I'm gonna go to Sophie's tomorrow after work. I'm not trying to get the whole place furnished by the time Mom and Dad arrive, but a couple of things might be nice. Sophie said the finish on the walls will be done by Monday."

"You'll fall in love with her store. Once I step inside, I never want to leave. I'd offer to come, but I'm going to the library. That guest speaker about matchmaking and relationships is going to be there tomorrow, and I volunteered to help Jewels with the setup."

"Ooh, maybe I'll stop by after. Wasn't it about navigating the dating world through social media?" I laughed. "I could learn the psychology behind Nick."

"Doubtful," she teased, turning out the back room light. "Ready?"

I gave a quick nod and grabbed my purse.

"You really did figure out a wonderful way to spend your time," I told my sister as we walked outside. She stopped to lock up the front door, and I rearranged the burnt orange chrysanthemums and propped up one of the pumpkins that took a tumble.

"Why, thank you." She chuckled and glanced toward her car. "I'm gonna run to the store before stopping by your house. Do you need anything?"

"Nah. I'm all set." I gave her a quick hug and she marched across the street. I'd parked down the road, and the walk to my car was quick, especially with the cold sea breeze winding up from the water.

I climbed into my Fiat and blasted the heater all the way to the house. It wasn't until I turned into my driveway and saw Nick hanging out on the porch that my stomach did an all-out gymnastic routine. The flutters only worsened once I parked and hopped out of the car to blaring music.

"Dear God. What is that sound?" I chuckled as Night Ranger's *Sister Christian* pumped from my house and Nick stood grinning under the porch light.

"The *good* eighties stuff." Nick's lips tugged into a half-smile.

Anthony walked outside and waved.

"Place looks a million times better inside." He bent over, but before he reappeared, white lights blinked on all around my house.

"What the heck?" I asked, in complete awe of the twinkling glow around the door, each window and the eaves.

"It sounded like the more sparkly distractions

we could put around your house, the better for your parents." Nick hopped down the steps and made his way over. "We have to make you look settled and well-adjusted, after all."

I couldn't believe he remembered what I'd said.

My sister's car pulled into my driveway and I glanced behind me. The headlights nearly blinded me as I raised my arm. She turned off her car and climbed out, jaw open as she walked toward me.

"Nick surprised me," I said in a near-whisper.

"I see that."

I turned back to see Nick motioning for me to come inside. He turned down the music, and the instant I stepped inside, I was nearly speechless. Even without whitewashing the clapboard, the place looked amazing, even better than I imagined.

"You guys are amazing. I think I'll be making you dinners for a year. I can't wait to go to Sophie's tomorrow after work. There's hope for my tiny cabin."

"Let me take you there," Nick said. "I have a truck."

Maddie couldn't hide her amusement, and I wondered if maybe she was noticing that Nick had several sides.

"I'd love that."

Nick squeezed me, and Anthony threw his signature smile in my direction. "Sophie can't wait to get her hands on this place. I'll tell her you'll be at the store. I know she'll want to be there."

"You guys are just incredible." I sighed just as a set of headlights lit up my house. I turned and craned my neck to see a car backing up into Nick's driveway.

"That's weird. I'm not expecting anyone," he grumbled.

I shot Maddie a look, and her gaze went to the floor.

"I think Andrea's hoping to make her holiday dreams come true." I half-laughed.

Nick's arm dropped from my waist and he froze.

"Andrea?" he asked, surprised the name rolled from my lips.

"That was her name, right?" I looked at my sister and she nodded. "Yeah, it almost sounded like this vacation was solely built on running into you, or apparently, pulling into your driveway."

Nick let out a sigh and rubbed the back of his neck.

"She came into the tea store today. Mentioned she had an old boyfriend here. Once she said it was Nick—" My sister stopped talking when she saw the pained look on Nick's face.

"Maybe you should stay here at Holly's until the car leaves," Anthony offered, glancing in my direction.

My hope was that Nick would agree.

He didn't.

"Nah. I need to go face whatever's going on." He looked down at me and grinned, knocking my shoulder with a fist that clearly landed me back into friend zone. "I'll pick you up at the shop tomorrow after work."

"Okay." I nodded and watched Anthony and Nick walk out of my house before letting out a long groan.

"It's probably for the best," Maddie said, but I knew she was as pissed about it as me.

"Yeah, totally." I twisted my face into a look of annoyance. "Amazing how easy it is to misjudge a kind gesture from the opposite sex. I totally took the Christmas lights as a shout out to get busy later tonight."

My sister laughed, but neither of us could ignore the truth in that statement.

"At least I got the walls stripped. I mean, that in itself is pretty cool. Totally worth the downgrade from dating material to friend material." I nodded, trying to persuade myself.

"Exactly, and way less hassle," she agreed.

I kept looking out the window, hoping to see Andrea's car pull away because he chased her off, but all I saw was Anthony drive away, and I knew the best thing to do was not look out the windows until morning.

Chapter Nine

"**A**nd so it begins." Maddie sighed, holding the back of her hand to her forehead, pretending like she's going to faint.

"What?"

She slid her phone across the counter, and I glanced down at the chain of texts from mom.

Should we stop on the way to your house to grab anything? Sheets, pillows, shampoo, conditioner, soap, nonfat milk, chocolate chip cookies?

I brought my eyes to my sister's before continuing to read the texts.

"That is so passive-aggressive." I started laughing.

"I know." My sister chuckled. "Why not just tell me this is what you want at the house before you arrive? And like I wouldn't have sheets for them, or pillows? We're how old? Just wait until you get to the bottom message."

I looked back down at her phone and began reading the text messages aloud.

Have you had time to order an arrangement for the table?

Are we doing turkey and also ham this year?

Do you need Aunt Hillary's Jell-O recipe?

Can I bring Muppet? The pet lodge is full.

I brought my head up slowly to see Maddie's perplexed expression.

"She wants to bring her cockatoo?" I asked. "I didn't even know you could bring birds on planes."

"Learn something new every day." She rested her head in her hands. "It's not like I can say no."

"I just feel so sorry for the people on the plane with Muppet. It's an angry bird. Nothing makes it happy. Can you imagine what it's going to do when Mom stuffs it in a cage and puts it under the seat in front of her?"

I started flapping my arms and making bird noises, and Maddie started laughing.

We were in this together.

"So tea drinkers do have all the fun," a

woman's voice said from the front of the store. I turned around, horrified, to see a brunette dressed in an apron, smiling at me.

My sister and I were having so much fun, we didn't even hear the jingle of the bell.

My cheeks flamed and I slid my damp palms along my pants.

"Hey, Natty," my sister said, waving.

"Natty?" I asked, snapping my head back to my sister.

"Yup. That's me." Natty grinned, holding an empty mug. "I was hoping to order some tea for the shop and also get a cup to tide me over. I have a huge floral order I need to get done before I can go home." Natty grinned, her eyes settling on me. "I had no idea I'd get a show though. Are you Holly?"

"I am." I nodded, hoping to erase the embarrassment from seconds before. "I was just mimicking our parents' bird. I don't usually look like I need to be committed."

"Long story," Maddie added, and Natty laughed.

"I've heard so much about you." Natty came in for a hug, and I looked over at my sister, who was shaking her head as if she had no idea what Natty was talking about. "Promise me you still have the holiday teas."

"Absolutely," Maddie said, coming around to grab Natty's mug. "What are you thinking about for your store?"

"Don't you own the floral shop?" I asked, remembering what Nick said about her.

"She also has a coffee stand inside," Maddie informed me.

"And I can't keep the gingerbread tea in stock," Natty said, wandering over to the shelves.

I glanced behind me at my sister, who couldn't keep her smile hidden. So my sister knew all of Nick's best friends. I guess it would make sense, considering the island's as small as a postage stamp.

I walked over to Natty and reached for the newest batch and our latest concoction. I lifted the lid and sniffed it.

"This is sugar cookie. It's my total favorite now. It reminds me of the Strawberry Shortcake dolls, for some reason."

Natty grinned and took the canister. "Oh. My. Gawd. It totally does. This has to come back with me."

"I'd be hooked up to the stuff if I could." I nodded in agreement. "I can't wait to come see your floral shop. I've been so focused on getting my little place done that I haven't had much time for exploring."

"Anytime. I also have pastries I always mark down this time of the day."

My brows shot up. "Really? I'm all about the sweets."

"Me too." Natty began trying out other teas, and I wandered to the back room. Nick might be here any second . . . or not.

I was hoping our plans were still on, but after Andrea's surprise appearance on the island, I had no idea what was going on in the Nick department.

"Did you hear that?" My sister asked, poking her head into the back room.

"No. Hear what? Is Nick here?"

My sister smiled and shook her head, motioning for me to come back out into the shop.

"What's up?" I asked.

"Tell her," Maddie said, eyeing Natty.

"Tell me what?" I sat on a stool and took a sip of the sugar cookie tea.

"You know that huge snowstorm we had?" Natty asked.

I nodded.

"Well, my fiancé, Cole, was out of town and the power went out. Next thing I knew, Nick was at my door."

"Nick?" I said softly, trying to amp the volume.

"Yup. Anyway, he brought me back to his house. Since he has a generator, he wanted me to be warm and snug." She was watching me carefully for a reaction.

"Did he tell you to say that?" I asked.

"Nope." She grinned. "I tried to convince him to have you come over, but he said you were too independent and would probably get offended."

I laughed. "Yes, I always get offended when it comes to hot water and heat." I fiddled with a pad of paper on the counter. "Although, I probably do confuse the hell out of him."

"You?" My sister laughed. "Never."

Natty's expression brightened and she sat a couple more canisters on the counter.

"So it was you that night?" I swallowed down

the excitement and tried to sound calm. "In his truck?"

"Indeed it was. Does that change things?"

"Now that Andrea's back on the island, I'm not sure it does, actually." I scowled.

Natty let out a gasp, and her face scrunched as if she'd just eaten a lemon. "I didn't hear that news."

"It just happened yesterday," Maddie informed her. "She stopped by with a group of friends." She leaned across the counter. "And then last night, when I was at Holly's with Nick and Anthony, the chick had the nerve to show up at Nick's house."

"You're kidding." Natty sounded disgusted, and I suddenly liked her even more.

I shook my head. "It's true. Not that it's any of my business, but I thought he didn't do relationships." I stared at Natty, hoping for some insight.

"He doesn't. At least, not relationships that work out well. Andrea was one of the few women he'd dated for a brief amount of time. We all despised her."

I hated that my heart smiled at that revelation.

"She was beyond demanding. To be honest, I didn't even think she liked him. She just used him. I was so relieved when they broke up. I can't imagine why she's back here."

My body relaxed, which was crazy because it wasn't like I was invested in Nick or any of his relationships. It wasn't my business.

"She seemed to think he would do her body

good," Maddie grumbled, and Natty laughed.

"Poor Nick. It's a blessing and a curse." Natty seemed tickled to reveal that bit of information. "Not that I have firsthand knowledge, but it's one of those things that doesn't stay quiet."

"Ha." I kept my gaze in front of me. "No man is *that* good. What was it Andrea's friend said though? Nick ruined her for others?"

"Probably true." Natty chuckled. "You know how he is a really kind and generous neighbor?"

My face burned and I didn't offer a reply.

"Well, from what I've heard, he's that way through and through."

My sister looked at her phone and groaned while I stood dizzied with the thought of living across from a man who was not only good-looking but magical in bed.

Ugh.

"What's wrong?" Natty asked, turning her attention to my sister.

"Our parents are coming for Thanksgiving," my sister muttered. "Which reminds me. I need to order an extravagant-looking Thanksgiving arrangement for our table."

Natty's brows shot up in surprise. "Okay. That's an unusual request."

"The bigger, the better." My sister rolled her eyes.

"Yes, if you could make it gaudy, that would be perfect," I added. "Maybe even incorporate a birdcage."

My sister laughed and shook her head. "Please don't."

Natty looked puzzled but happily agreed. "Do you want me to drop it off on Wednesday?"

Maddie nodded. "You're a lifesaver."

"Absolutely. But you have to tell me what's up with the bird references."

"My parents are bringing their pet bird for Thanksgiving," I answered.

"You can do that?"

"Yep. I just need to make sure I don't cook the wrong bird."

"You wouldn't." I laughed.

"Depends if the thing squawks all night or not."

Natty laughed, and I slid off the stool. I forgot I had a few items left to put away in the back before I could take off to Sophie's with—or without—Nick.

"Well, don't worry about Andrea. I'm surprised he didn't mention it to me, but I'm sure he put her in her place," Natty said loudly so I could hear. "That relationship, if you could call it that, is a thing of the past."

Except that the car didn't leave for hours. Not that I was spying or anything.

"Thanks," I hollered back, sliding a box of brown paper sacks under a workbench and organizing the Christmas giftwrap we'd just received. "But we're just neighbors. If he wants to bang an ex, it's none of my beeswax. I'm not looking for a relationship, unless it's a temporary one to impress my parents. I might even convince Nick to help me with Tinder. Maybe he's got the right approach about relationships.

Although hearing he's that good in bed isn't what I need right now." I shoved the bows in the corner.

"But it might be fun to take him for a spin," I muttered under my breath.

I took a step back and admired the bright greens, sparkly reds, and silver Christmas paper waiting for us to wrap presents for the next thirty days.

"You ready?" Nick asked from the doorway, and my heart literally fractured into a million little mortified pieces.

"You're here?" My eyes widened in horror as I turned around to face him.

"Wasn't I supposed to be?" He slid his phone out of his pocket. "Did I miss a text or something? Did the plans change?"

"No. Yes. I mean . . ." I sputtered, took a deep breath, and stood up straighter. "Yes, you're right on time."

He suppressed a grin, and I knew for certain he'd heard every word.

"Awesome. Well, I'm gonna go help Natty take her stuff to the store and grab one of her pastries, and I'll meet you at my truck. I parked right out front so I can easily take you out for a spin. You want anything?"

Please, oh please, can I be swallowed into the earth never to return?

I opened my mouth to say something.

Anything.

But when that didn't happen, his smile widened.

"Ready, Natty?" he called behind him.

"Sure am," she replied. I looked through the door and saw that she only had a small bag. I brought my gaze back to Nick's, and I could tell he loved every second of what just happened. In fact, I was certain he was looping the words over and over again in his mind.

"Croissant," I blurted out, still frozen.

"Croissant coming up." He gave a slight nod and headed out with Natty.

Chapter Ten

"**W**ow."

"Wow what?" I asked my sister.

"I swear he's into you." Maddie wriggled her brows.

"Not exactly my cup-o-tea if he spent the night with Andrea," I nearly growled. "You know, her car was there for *hours* after you left."

"Maybe they were just talking."

"First of all, does that look like a man you just want to talk to? And second of all, she said it herself. She wants Nick."

"That doesn't mean he wants her."

"True, and the good news is that it doesn't matter either way. I'm old enough not to put too much stock into a kiss or a flirt." I grabbed my purse. "And now, I'm off to pick out furniture with a man who is turning into quite the sidekick."

"Fling some of that fire in his direction and you'll get really far." She laughed as she turned off the laptop and lights. "I'll see you tomorrow."

"Bright and early." I waved and walked outside to the crisp air.

Nick was already at his truck, smiling, as I adjusted my red wool sweater.

"Red's a good color on you. Between that bra and this . . ." He opened the door for me and I climbed in. "You've got a lock on the color."

"I don't think that's how it works." I flashed a smile. "But thanks."

He shut the door, and I watched him walk around the front of his truck. He seemed so laid back and confident. He reminded me of one of those guys who just sits back on a bench, relaxed, watching the world go by. Nick didn't strike me as a city guy, regardless of how much time he spent in Seattle.

I looked around the cab. It was a nice truck, probably less than a year old because it still had that new-car smell. Nick opened his door and climbed in. Once he shut the door, it was like this tiny space magnified his maleness, if that was even a thing, but I wasn't going to fall for it. If there was one thing about Nick, it would be that he needed to work for something in his life when it involved the female species. He'd obviously had it too easy.

"So did you get everything you needed from Andrea last night?" I teased.

He'd just pulled the truck onto the main

street.

"I didn't need anything from her. I didn't want anything from her." He smiled and glanced at me.

"Well, I'm sure she's going to be hurt if you don't invite her over for Thanksgiving. She's been looking forward to this island trip for quite a long time, by the sounds of it, and she certainly wasn't shy about expressing *her* need at our tea shop."

"Is that so?"

"Yup." The cab was getting hot. I looked at the dials for the heat, but they were centered in the middle, so I opened the window.

"What were her needs?" he asked, purely amused.

"You. You seemed to be the need she had. I personally can't imagine *needing* something so badly, but at least you were on hand to meet it."

He laughed, which only annoyed me. I half expected him to give me a one-liner.

"What? It's not like her visit was only a few minutes long once you got to your house. I know what happened behind those closed doors." I winked at him.

He pulled into the parking lot and found the last empty spot in front of the store.

"This is so cute," I said, trying to change the subject.

Blinking twinkle lights in the thousands had been wrapped around the two front posts, and a rustic bench sat by the front door. The window displays made me think of nestling in my cabin with a piping-hot cup of tea and a blanket. This was going to be my splurge for sure.

Nick unbuckled and turned in his seat.

"Believe it or not, I don't make a habit of sleeping with exes."

"It's honestly not my business whether you do or don't. I'm happy for you or anyone who can make a love connection." I wiggled my brows.

"There is no love connection with Andrea. We just talked."

I tapped his knee sympathetically. "I'm sorry."

He let out an exasperated groan.

"I explained to her that whatever she's been spreading around town isn't appreciated." His expression softened as he watched me.

"It took you two hours to explain that?"

He frowned. "No. It took two hours to get her to stop crying."

"It did not."

"Seriously." He shook his head. "The kicker is that she doesn't even like me. They were crocodile tears."

"How could someone not like you?" I asked in surprise. "You're one of the most likable people I've ever met."

"Thanks for that, but it's true."

"So she just wants you for your body?" I joked. "The pressure."

"Appears to be the case," he said, completely deadpan.

"The life of a playboy." I shook my head. "Must be exhausting, fighting 'em off with a stick and breaking hearts right before the holidays."

"You're not upset?" he asked.

"Why would I be upset?" I slid my hand to the door. "You're a sexy neighbor with a sordid past. It makes for interesting spying and good conversation at the store. You're not mine to claim." I cleared my throat. "Or vice versa."

"You talk about me at the store?"

"Only when you give me something to talk about. Anyway, let's get inside. I've got a house to make presentable and only days to do it. Sophie said her team was ahead of schedule and the walls will be done tomorrow. That girl knows how to get things done."

"That is the truth."

I slid out of the truck and waited for Nick, who was moseying on over in his gray plaid flannel shirt and loose jeans without a care in the world.

This guy had it made.

"If you find something you want, we can always take it home tonight, and I can keep it in my garage until your place is done tomorrow," he told me as he opened the door for me.

"That's sweet of you."

I walked inside and was immediately hit with the smell of hot apple cider. The store was like a winter wonderland. I'd never seen a store like this in my life. Room displays stretched as far as my eye could see, but they were so realistic and inviting it felt like I was in someone's home for the holidays already.

I wanted everything.

"Wow. Can I just have it all?"

"It might get a little crowded." He grinned. "Sophie's a talented lady. To top it all off, all the signs, wreaths, and arrangements are her own designs."

"I feel like I've died and gone to heaven. This is exactly how I imagined my cabin to be." I walked over to a beautiful oversized chair that looked like it could fit two to three people comfortably.

Nick laughed as I sank into the overstuffed red velvet cushion. The light pine armrests were lightly distressed.

"What?" I asked, sinking in deeper.

"You like it?"

"Like it? Gotta have it. Wouldn't it be perfect in the main room?" I asked, slowly getting up from the chair.

"It would look pretty great," he agreed, nodding with a sparkle in his eyes as I grabbed a few throw pillows resting on a coffee table.

"And these are the perfect pillows," I said, searching for the price tag. The white and red plaid was so crisp and clean.

"Hi, you two," Sophie said, coming from somewhere in the back.

"I'm in love and I've only made it in ten feet."

"That's what I love to hear." She eyed the pillows I was holding. "Wouldn't those look cute in that chair? I could see this in your place." Sophie eyed a silver vase that came up to my waist. "And this with some curly willow right by the window would really set the corner off and the view of the woods. Don't you think?"

"I can hardly contain my excitement." I hopped on my toes. "I'm in love with that chair, and it's the most comfortable chair I've ever sat on." I glanced at Nick. "No offense."

"None taken." He held up his hands and Sophie laughed.

"I wanted to show you this dining table. It seats four but also has a leaf that extends it to six." She walked over to a rustic table with thick planks of weathered dark wood. "It's compact but versatile."

"I love it. I wasn't thinking about the dining table yet, but it matches that chair perfectly."

"It does." Sophie nodded.

I slid my hand along the wood, feeling the nicks and grain of the wood. "I definitely want this table and that chair."

I turned to Nick. "I think that will be enough for when my parents come out. What about you?"

"Totally. Just enough to give them the impression they can find a place to sit until you steal the one chair."

"So maybe a couch too?" I laughed.

"Only if you want them to be comfortable."

"Not sure I do." I scowled. "That's what my sister's house is for."

"I can't wait to meet these two." Nick chuckled.

"Who said you were going to?" My brow arched.

"You can't turn away a neighbor who's trying to make a pie and needs sugar, right?"

"That'll happen." I shook my head and followed Sophie through the store, stopping every so often to admire one of her designs.

By the time I left, I'd managed to purchase the oversized chair, a dining set, a small brown leather sofa, end tables, a coffee table, a tall vase, and several items for the walls. Sophie insisted on throwing in the pillows, which was certainly sweet of her. By the time Nick loaded up the truck with the chair and coffee table, I was fully prepared for my parents to come to town. In fact, I was kind of looking forward to it.

Nick and I were going to come back for the rest of the stuff tomorrow, and I was thoroughly excited about making my house a home.

He dropped me off at my car at the shop, and when I got home, I saw him in my driveway already unstrapping the chair and coffee table from his truck. He'd gotten a dolly from his house to move the furniture in.

I pulled in front of my cabin and saw my twinkle lights already blinking away.

This really was home.

Nearly jumping out of the car, I felt my pulse race as I watched him move the coffee table onto the dolly.

"I'm not kidding when I say you're the best neighbor in the world."

"Sophie said they only have the bedroom and hallway left, so I thought we could put this inside so you don't have to hang out on your lawn chair anymore."

"Hey, the lawn chair is only for special occasions. Usually, I just sit on the floor."

"Exactly."

"I'm so in love with this chair," I said, caressing the wood.

"I'm glad you like it."

"Like it? I'm not kidding when I say love it. I'll probably sleep in it until I pick out a bed."

"You don't have a bed yet?" He asked, surprise filling his face.

"No." I shook my head. "I've been sleeping on a cot."

"And you're still this perky?" He began rolling the coffee table toward the door, and I jogged in front of him to open my door.

"Yup. What can I say?"

"Anthony did your bedroom while I hung the Christmas lights so I've never been in it." I watched him maneuver the coffee table up the steps, attempting to lend a hand when I could as he wheeled it by me.

"Are you looking for an invitation?"

Amusement shined through his eyes as he wheeled the coffee table by.

"So since you're not making Andrea's Thanksgiving dreams come true, what are you up to?" I asked as he placed the coffee table in the room.

"Natty and Cole are hosting, so Sophie, Anthony, Jewels, and Jake are all going to be there. It should be fun."

"That'll be nice."

"Should be." He nodded, standing with the dolly.

"Think about us while you're enjoying your meal. We'll be trying to entertain my parents and their bird."

"They're bringing a bird?"

"I didn't even know people could travel with them, but yeah. Muppet will be joining us all while we eat turkey."

"I would like to see who your parents are." He studied me.

"What's that supposed to mean?" I placed my hands on my hips.

"Just curious."

"Hmph. Do you want a hard apple cider?" I asked.

"Sure. I might need it to get the chair inside. It was a real bitch getting it to Sophie's."

"What do you mean?" I asked, the realization slowly dawning on me.

"You somehow beelined to all my furniture in her store." He grinned proudly. "There are a lot of other manufacturers, but I'm happy to say you've got amazing taste."

I warmed instantly.

"Wow, and you didn't say a word?"

"I didn't want to influence you, but I'm pretty happy you're the one who wound up with some of my favorite pieces."

I shook my head. "Incredible."

I took two ciders out of the fridge and handed him one.

"You know what I think is incredible?" he asked.

"What's that?"

"That kiss the other night."

"It certainly made an impression," I muttered.

Nicks eyes narrowed on me as he took a slow sip of his cider. His dark hair fell across his brows and I couldn't handle it anymore.

"Just tell me this." I folded my arms across my chest. "Do you realize how sexy you are, or is this nonchalant act just that? An act?"

"You think I'm sexy?" A smile slid across his lips.

"Doesn't the world?"

"I don't know." He shrugged. "So does that mean you liked the kiss? Because I haven't been able to get it—or you—out of my head since."

Chapter Eleven

"But we want to see your cabin. We'll be at Maddie's the rest of the week. We've got plenty of time to settle in here." Muppet was sitting on my mom's shoulder, and my dad just nodded in agreement. "I just want to see why you chose to be in the middle of the woods instead of in a town, like your sister."

And so it began.

My parents had arrived at my sister's right on time. It was the Tuesday before Thanksgiving, and the week already went into slow motion.

It didn't help that I couldn't get Nick out of my head. He'd helped bring home the rest of the items, and Sophie came over last night to help me arrange my furniture, hang the décor, and add a couple of rugs I'd picked out. I actually wanted nothing more than to be in my cozy little cabin with a nosy neighbor popping in now and again.

"Mom, the island is pretty small. It's not like I'm three hours from here." I glanced at my sister. "What is it? Like fifteen minutes away?"

"If that." My sister nodded, smiling painfully.

"Maddie even has an early dinner for you guys since you've been traveling all day. Why not just stay the night and come over in the morning?" I suggested.

"Nonsense. The dinner will keep, won't it, Maddie?"

"Whatever you want to do." Maddie sighed. "But the breadcrumbs will get soggy."

"I always thought breadcrumbs were a waste anyway." My mom flung her hands in the direction of the kitchen.

"Mom, I think you're kind of missing the point. The mac and cheese is extra tasty right out of the oven, and the oven is about to ding in ten minutes."

"Well, if you didn't live so far away, we could come and go and get back in plenty of time. Isn't that right, Barry?"

My dad nodded.

I bit my lip and blinked slowly. My mom's blonde hair skimmed her shoulders and a pink headband secured any loose strays. She wore a matching pink cardigan twinset and ivory slacks. The bird turned its head and stared at me.

I glanced at my parents' suitcases still in the entry.

"I'll take your bags upstairs," I muttered.

"Oh, thank you. Muppet's cage is still in the rental car. Keys are on that barrel thing your sister insists is a table."

"I assume that's my cue to go get it?" My lips puckered into a pout when I realized my mom felt that was an obvious unsaid and began nuzzling her bird.

Maddie rushed to my side and held in a giggle.

"Here, let me help you with these," she said, reaching for the biggest one.

"Why, thank you. That's so kind of you."

We hauled the suitcases upstairs and took a momentary breather before I ran outside to the car to bring in the cage. I was stunned to see how large it was for one bird. As I was finagling the home away from home for Muppet, my sister came up behind me and nearly scared me to death.

"Is it just me or is she worse than usual?" My sister hissed.

"I was thinking the same thing." I stumbled backward once the cage became free. "I owe you big time."

"It's just a shame the tea store is so busy the day before Thanksgiving or I'd be able to spend more time with them tomorrow." She flashed an evil grin.

"I thought we were closing early tomorrow." I chuckled.

"Not anymore."

As we walked into the house, the oven was chiming and my mom was petting her bird.

"How long has it been dinging?" I asked.

"Oh, just a couple of minutes," my dad assured me.

My sister scurried to the kitchen to take out the macaroni and cheese as I stood in the living room with the birdcage.

"Anywhere in particular you want this?" I asked.

"Away from the window. Muppet can't handle a draft, and this house is certainly old and drafty."

"Actually, the house has been completely reinsulated and the windows have all been replaced."

Unlike my home, so I can't wait to hear what she'll say about that.

"Let's put Muppet here." She moved a table directly in front of the television and smiled.

"But it will block the television." My brows knitted together in confusion.

"Muppet loves to watch TLC, and she's working on her vocabulary."

"Of course she is." I smiled and plopped the cage on the table.

"How often does Muppet stay in her cage?" I asked.

"She tells me when she wants private time." The bird nuzzled my mom's chin, and I glanced at my dad, who seemed to be in his own world.

"Makes sense." I nodded.

"Dinner's ready to eat now," Maddie said, poking her head around the corner. "Unless you want to head to Holly's first."

"Nope. I, for one, don't want soggy

breadcrumbs. Come on, Dad." I looped my arm around his and nearly dragged him into the kitchen. "Look how cute this table setting is."

"The candles are nice, but the flame might scare Muppet," my mom said, standing at the table, which was Dad's signal to blow them out.

"Muppet's going to be at the table?" I asked.

"Of course. Where else would Muppet be?"

"The cage?" I asked.

"No. She's feeling social right now. Muppet's had a long day of travel."

"It's best to just let the bird do what she wants. Then she doesn't spend the entire time squawking," my dad said, taking a seat at the table. "It's more peaceful that way."

I studied him, not sure if he was talking about Mom or Muppet.

"I've been craving mac and cheese since Maddie said she was making it this morning," I told Maddie, taking a seat next to Dad.

"It does smell good." My mom smiled.

Finally! The woman had something nice to say.

"It's just a shame you're always so rushed with owning your own business. You don't have time to really get in the kitchen and make a decent meal," my mom continued.

My jaw dropped to the table, but I was able to scrape it up as Maddie's eyes widened. Thanksgiving dinner was going to be so much fun.

"Some would be impressed that Maddie is a successful business woman who owns her own home, cooks dinner, entertains demanding out-of-town guests, and manages to do it all with a smile." I grinned a toothy grin.

"Oh, honey, I didn't mean to imply that what your sister has accomplished isn't special. I just wish she had someone to share it with." She took a bite of the pasta. "This is delicious, though."

"Even for a casserole?" I asked dryly.

"Exactly." My mom nodded.

"It's amazing." My sister yawned. "It's not even six o'clock and I'm exhausted."

"I bet you are." I nodded. "This is the best mac and cheese ever, Sis."

Maddie took a bite and moaned. "It is pretty good."

I glanced over at my mom, my sister's gaze following.

"Uh, Mom," I whispered.

"Yes, dear?" She asked, taking a bite.

"Is Muppet potty-trained?"

"Don't be silly. She's a bird."

"Obviously." My sister chuckled. My dad glanced at my mom's shoulder and rolled his eyes.

"Muppet shit on your shoulder again." Dad kept eating.

I think in this instance, what blew me away were two things.

The first was that not only did my dad keep eating, but so did my mom. It literally would make my head explode if I thought about it too long, so I just slid my plate closer to me and kept munching while my sister kept in more laughter.

The second thing I noticed was far more

chilling.

I didn't want to become like my parents. I didn't want to be married to someone who was okay with me sitting at a dinner table with shit on my shoulder.

I didn't want a marriage to be a marathon unless both people were actively participating. For the first time ever, I realized my dad had checked out. When? I didn't know, but he was long gone. What bothered me even more than his not being present was that was that my mom hadn't even noticed.

So here we sat, a few days before Thanksgiving, as a family pretending to be something we weren't. This wasn't exactly the revelation I wanted to unfold.

No. I liked believing that my parents were not only in it for the long haul, but that they were enjoying the years that passed by. How did I not see this, or was it a recent development?

A chill shot through me. Maybe I recognized this about my parents for longer than I realized.

But they'd been married for thirty-seven years. It felt like the room was getting tinier by the second. I looked over at Maddie, and it was like she'd just been hit in the head with the same thought as me.

Suddenly, the idea of taking them to my cabin didn't seem so bad. Anything to shake up this mood settling around the table. Maybe that was all I was noticing. Maybe they were tired from all the travel. Goodness knows, traveling with a feathered pet couldn't be easy.

After my mom finished her meal, she got up and rinsed her plate with Muppet still firmly planted on her shoulder.

"This was an amazing meal," my dad said, sitting back in the chair.

"Glad you liked it," Maddie said, smiling.

"Do you still want to go to the cabin?" I asked.

"Absolutely," my mom said. "Just let me change and toss this in the washing machine."

Muppet started squawking, and I was actually grateful for the interruption. Once my mom made her way up the stairs, I glanced at my sister, who was finishing her last couple of bites.

"Is everything okay with you guys?" I asked my dad.

"Totally fine. Why do you ask?" He scowled.

"Things just seem . . . different. Mom's more uptight than usual, and I think she's obsessed." I kept my eyes on my dad, and his expression fell.

"I hate that bird," my dad grumbled. "I'm about to retire, and now I have to share our house with a cackling cockatoo. She treats that thing better than me."

"Have you told her how you feel?" I asked, glancing at my sister.

"And sound like a man jealous of a bird?" He shook his head. "I'd like to keep what little dignity I have to myself, if nothing else."

"She does seem to be preoccupied," I agreed.

"It's crazy. She walks the bird more than anyone has ever walked a dog. She cuddles it and talks to it. I used to think she was talking to me, and now I know better. I love your mother more than life itself, but Muppet has got to learn her place."

My sister giggled.

"You need to talk to Mom," my sister said. "Cockatoos live for a very long time."

Dad let out a sigh. "We'll see about that."

"I'm ready," my mom called from the foyer.

Muppet was sitting on my mom's shoulder, waiting for our response.

"Mom, I think you should leave Muppet here."

"Absolutely not."

"Please?" I asked. "I just got the floors done and I have new furniture. I already saw what the bird did to your clothes."

"It's Holly's house," my dad agreed. "If she doesn't want you to bring Muppet, respect her wishes."

"Why didn't anyone worry about that for my house?" Maddie laughed as we moved out of the kitchen. "I didn't get an option to keep Muppet in Illinois."

My mom looked disgruntled but didn't argue. Instead, she placed Muppet in the oversized birdcage and gave it kisses.

"Maybe it's too late at night," my mom offered. "You were right. We can go see your house tomorrow."

I shook my head. "Nope. You wanted to see my place, you get to see it. Muppet will be fine."

My dad grinned, knowing he'd get a few minutes' peace without the bird.

"Fine." My mom strapped her purse over her shoulder and glanced at my sister, who had already put on her coat.

"I'll meet you over there," I told them, giving my dad a hug.

"We're not all riding over together?" my mom asked.

I gave her a quick kiss.

"Nope. I'm not coming back here tonight. I'll be staying at my place." I slid a look at my sister, who was grinning.

"See you there, honey."

"See ya." I bounded out of the house, excited to get back to my home. Since it had been finished, I'd barely been able to spend time in it.

Halfway to my house, a downpour began and I really couldn't wait to snuggle inside.

I pulled into my driveway, darted out of my car, dashed up the steps to my house, plugged in the Christmas lights, put on some Christmas music, and lit a fire in the fireplace to take the chill off my house. I barely had time to put my purse in my bedroom before they knocked on the front door.

Except that when I opened the door, it wasn't my family staring at me. It was Nick.

"Saw your lights and solo car in the drive and thought you might like some company." His devilish grin nearly did me in, but headlights that came up behind him quickly dashed those hopes.

"My parents wanted to see my house." I smiled and nodded toward the car that pulled up.

"My timing is impeccable." His brow arched.

"You know, we could probably use some

levity."

"What is that supposed to mean?" he asked, gliding into the room.

"My parents are acting weird. My dad blames my mom's new pet."

"The bird?" he asked, and I nodded.

"He feels she spends more time with her feathered friend and gives it more attention than him. He's probably right."

"Now that is a marital issue you don't hear every day." He grinned and brushed away a piece of stray hair that caught in my eyelashes.

His gaze fastened on mine and a shiver ran down my spine, which I quickly shook off.

"There's definitely more behind it, but that's all I've managed to piece together so far," I told him.

"Maybe they just need to spend some time together away from the bird," he suggested.

"Agreed, but my mom almost had a fit that Muppet couldn't come over tonight." I shook my head. "Very weird."

I heard the car doors shut, one at a time, and took a deep breath.

"What does your dad do for a living?"

"He's worked for the same company for twenty-five years. Honestly, he always traveled a lot, so I think my mom got used to building a life without him, but he's going to be retiring soon."

I glanced out my window.

"I think Muppet is her way to get back at him for all the times he was away."

"You think?" I whispered, watching them

trundle toward the porch.

"It's just a guess."

I opened the door before they had a chance to knock, and my mom's eyes immediately gravitated to Nick.

"Who is this?" my mom asked, a smile spreading across her lips.

"This is my pesky neighbor from across the street. His name's Nick."

My dad smiled and nodded, taking Nick's hand and shaking it.

"Nice to meet you," my dad said, coming inside my home. "It's nice to know she's got someone across the street to look out for her."

"I do my best," Nick said, grinning.

I punched his arm and he didn't even flinch.

It was actually nice to have Nick here as a distraction. Instead of my mom picking apart my home, she was focusing on the man in front of her.

"Are you single?" my mom asked as Maddie shut the door and sighed loudly.

"You can't get any more single than Nick," I said.

My mom looked around the room as silence filled the space.

I loved everything about my little cabin, and I really hoped that whatever was about to come out of her mouth didn't make me regret having them over tonight.

"The furniture is lovely," my mom said, craning her neck to get a better look at the chair. "It fits perfectly."

It felt like the biggest weight had been lifted, and I let out a huge sigh of relief as Nick squeezed my shoulder.

"Thank you. Nick actually designed and built the furniture."

"You're a talented young man," my father said, and I stifled a laugh. Nick was well into his thirties.

"Thanks. I've been lucky to find customers."

"This isn't luck, son. This is talent," my dad said, walking over to the coffee table.

"The man knows how to use power tools." My sister laughed, and I shot her a death stare.

"Well, I had my worries about you picking up and moving clear across the country, but I have to say this place is as cute as a button." My mom smiled and held out her arms for a hug.

She was back to her old self.

"Thanks, Mom. I love it here." I squeezed her back. "I still have more to do, but it already feels like home."

"You never struck me as a city girl," my mom said, taking a step back before eyeing Nick. "You always reminded me of someone who would excel in a small town."

My sister chuckled behind me. Mom was up to her old tricks.

"I think this place might be a little too small to raise a family, but it certainly fits you now."

"Thanks, Mom," I grumbled, feeling like I was in third grade. "Anyway, would anyone like a slice of pie? I bought blackberry."

"I'd love some." Dad rubbed his hands

together before pinching my mom's rear, and Nick's eyes widened.

"Great. I'll dish us up some." I walked past Nick, and as his hand slid to do the same, I smacked him.

"Do you have any plans for tomorrow?" Nick asked my parents.

"We were just going to walk around town," my mom informed him. "Take in the sights."

"Do you like being on the water?" Nick asked.

"We do." My dad nodded.

"Well, one of my good buddies has a boat, and I know he'd love to take you around tomorrow, show you some of the coves we're famous for. The weather's supposed to be great for sailing. Chilly, but calm." Nick glanced at me, and I couldn't help but feel that familiar flutter.

My mom and dad looked at each other, and my mom nodded. "That would actually be a lot of fun."

"You wouldn't be able to take Muppet," Maddie told her.

"I know that." My mom furrowed her brows like it was my sister who was the crazy one.

"My friend actually rents his boat for overnight stays in the harbor too. Anyway, I'll give him a call. When I spoke with him this morning, he still had an opening."

"That's so sweet of you." I walked the pie over to the dining table while my parents took a seat, and I could hear them excitedly talking about the next day's adventures. Nick was a miracle worker. "Would you like a slice?"

He was already at the door with the phone to his ear to call his friend. He shook his head and closed the door behind him. I watched him pace along the porch, smiling and laughing as he spoke to his friend.

"He's a really nice man," my mom said, taking the first bite of pie.

"He is." I nodded in agreement. "There isn't a mean bone in his body."

My mom's eyes stayed on mine as I took a bite of the pie.

"What?" I asked, trying to slide all emotion from my expression.

"Nothing, dear."

I glanced out the window, and Nick motioned for me to come on the porch.

"I'll be right back," I told my family before scooting outside.

I motioned for him to move away from the window, which he did.

"It's all set." He grinned. "My friend is going to make it special, romantic. We'll get the fire back between those two."

"That was really sweet of you." I looked up into his gaze.

"I'd imagine it takes the pressure off you and your sister too."

"You have no idea."

"Oh, I think I do. Your mom's on her best behavior."

"You can tell?"

"Yup."

"Do you want to come in for some pie?" I

pointed behind me, and Nick smiled.

"I'm good. Enjoy your family while they're here. Jack will be at dock in the main marina at eleven tomorrow. If you need anything over the holiday, let me know." His eyes fell to my lips, and I swallowed down the desire to feel his mouth against mine again.

"Okay," I nearly whispered. "If you want to stop by my sister's house on turkey day, you're more than welcome."

"Thanks."

"No, thank *you*." I grinned. "I love my chair."

He looked like he wanted to say something else, but instead, he took a deep breath and kissed the top of my head.

"I love that you love it." He turned around and walked down my steps. "See ya around."

Chapter Twelve

"**D**o the gods hate me?" my sister squealed into the phone.

"Just take a deep breath," I told her, having no idea what could have gone wrong so early in the morning on Thanksgiving. "The gods don't hate you. They love you, which is why Nick knew of a way to keep the parents entertained yesterday."

She groaned. "This is bad."

"Did you accidentally season Muppet and put her in the oven?"

My sister laughed. "No."

"Then everything's going to be just fine."

"A pipe broke and my kitchen is flooded."

I froze. She'd done so much to her cute little kitchen—new floors and cabinets.

"I'll be right over." I almost hung up on her,

but she stopped me.

"I've already got the water turned off, and some twenty-four-hour emergency service is here vacuuming up the water and getting the fans in to dry it out."

"I'm so sorry. What can I do to help?"

"Mom and Dad are out on a walk with Muppet." There was silence. "Can we have Thanksgiving at your place?"

"Of course. I wouldn't have it any other way. Do you want me to come over to help bring the food over to cook?"

"Nah. We can handle it, but I have to bring the bird."

"Well, of course you have to bring the bird. I'll cook it at the house."

My sister giggled. "Not that bird. That's a given. Muppet. With all the doors and windows open and the fans going, Muppet would probably get sick."

I wasn't heartless. I actually loved animals. I didn't even mind Muppet. I just didn't understand how my mom was acting around the bird.

Maybe Nick was more right than I knew.

"No problem. Whatever you need help with, I'll do it. I'll go make a place in my bedroom for the bird. That way we can shut the door." I took in a breath. "But are you okay?"

"I'm fine."

I heard my mom's voice in the background, followed by a squawking mess.

"I'll let you go. Come on over. I'll be ready and

waiting to cut celery and chop nuts, but I'm still in pjs."

"Okay. See ya soon."

"Love ya." I hung up and looked around my little place.

Truth be told, I was kind of excited to host my first holiday. I wish it wasn't because my sister's kitchen experienced a tidal wave, but it would be fun—Muppet and all.

I went into my bedroom, moved the cot to the wall, and shoved a few boxes into the closet. I didn't want birdseed to get in my sheets or work its way into the boxes of clothes I still needed to unpack. I scanned the mostly empty room. It looked sad but fine for Muppet. Maybe I should bring a radio in for the cockatoo. I definitely needed to make this the next room I concentrated on.

The bedroom window faced the front of the house, and I had an urge to look out the window toward Nick's place. I stood on my toes and tried to see his house through the trees. I was actually surprised to see part of his roofline behind the workshop. I craned my neck and saw his truck in his driveway. I wondered when he'd be headed to Natty's house. It was nice that they had such a tight group of friends. I'd never really experienced that before. I guess that was why it was so easy to leave it all behind in New York.

I walked into the living room, turned on my stereo, and *Heaven is a Place on Earth* blared through the speakers.

My shoulders sagged. I really was stuck in the

eighties.

But who cares?

I started singing at the top of my lungs as I tidied up my kitchen and got all the pots and pans that we might need out of the cabinets. My job had been to make the pumpkin pie, which I did last night, but I still had all the bowls left in the sink to clean, and then I'd be ready for the family.

I boogied my way to the sink with Belinda Carlisle singing with me, and I felt worlds away. As I scrubbed the dirty dishes, I thought about how much my life had changed. After getting let go from my job, I walked away from it all. New York was full of possibilities in the same line of work I specialized in, but I didn't care. I wanted out.

The problem was that I didn't know what I wanted to do next. Did I just want to spend my time at the tea shop with my sister or did I want to try something new?

But what would I even do? The idea of setting up a little investment service company on the island had popped in my head, but that wasn't exactly something I was itching to do.

I glanced over at my chair. Nick was lucky. He had a passion. He knew what he liked to do and he did it. I didn't have a clue about what I might like to do. All I did in New York was work, sleep, go out with a few coworkers now and again, and start the cycle all over again.

Yeah. There was a reason why I knew to leave that life behind.

I let out a groan as I dried off a bowl.

"Belinda Carlisle?" my sister asked, and I nearly dropped the bowl in fear. "That's not very holidayish."

"You scared the crap out of me." I laughed, my heart hammering in my chest.

"Well, you didn't exactly answer our knocks, so I used your spare key." She set a huge cardboard box on the counter with all kinds of bags of things inside and grabbed the stereo remote to turn down the music.

"Where's Mom and Dad?" I asked, drying off my hands.

"Dad's bringing in the floral arrangement and Mom's bringing in Muppet."

"Yay." I chuckled.

"Wait until you see the design Natty came up with for the flowers. Mom loved it. If she could get one sent to herself every week, I think she would." Maddie grinned.

"Happy Turkey Bird Day," Dad said, coming through the door with a monstrosity of an arrangement.

"It looks nothing like what Natty usually creates," my sister assured me.

"But it's perfection for Mom." I nodded, staring at the arrangement. How my dad even made it inside without tripping, I didn't know.

The piece was probably three feet long and was just as tall in the center. A pillar with an ivory candle atop had jewels in autumn colors dripping all around and orange, red, and yellow flowers sprang to life. It was gaudy and over the top.

"Is that a miniature bird cage?" I asked, squinting my eyes as Dad placed it in the center of my dining room table.

"That it is." Maddie laughed.

My mom came in with a quiet and grateful looking Muppet on her shoulder. The birdcage was in her left hand, but she came over to hug me with her right. Muppet eyed me funny, and I got a taste of what my father's been dealing with.

"Isn't that the most beautiful arrangement?" my mom asked. "A lot of talent seems to live on this island."

"Does seem that way." I nodded in agreement. "I made a place for Muppet in my bedroom. The room is pretty much empty because I haven't had time to fix it up, so don't judge."

"Would I ever do that?" my mom asked innocently.

"No. Never." Maddie chuckled as my mom followed me down the hall and into the mostly bare room.

"I thought you could put her in the corner so she could still see out the window."

"That's a perfect spot," my mom agreed, setting down the birdcage.

I glanced at her, surprised, since I expected her to put up a fuss about Muppet's location.

"So did you like the boat trip?" I asked. I worked in the shop all day yesterday, and it was actually swamped so I hadn't heard about anything since Tuesday.

"Your sister didn't tell you?"

I shook my head.

"We loved it. We actually spent the night on it last night."

I studied my mom, realizing she looked absolutely refreshed and less frantic about life.

"I didn't know that."

"Your friend, Nick, certainly is thoughtful."

I stared at her, bewildered.

"The boat ride was completely romantic. Red roses, candles, a violinist to serenade us through the evening . . ."

"Really? I had no idea."

"There was a chef who made us dinner, and the captain left, never to return. The boat had been reserved for us overnight. I didn't even know you could do that. Such a quaint spot you live in."

My mind spun wildly from what my mom relayed. How in the world did Nick plan all this for my parents?

And why?

"You were okay with leaving Muppet at Maddie's?" I asked.

My mom nodded. "I think I've been spending too much time with the bird. It's taken over my life."

"You don't say," I teased.

"Sometimes, love isn't perfect, and after this many years together, it's nice to have a reminder of what brought us together in the first place. Anyway, we signed up for another tour on Saturday."

"Really?" I owed Nick big time.

"Sure did. Do you know what Dad told me last night?"

"What?"

"He thought I was paying attention to Muppet to get back at him for all those years he spent traveling for his job."

"Well?"

She let out a sigh. "I think he might be right. How ridiculous is that?"

I shrugged. "It sounds like communication is opening up again between you two."

"More than that." My mom smiled and I cringed.

"I love you, but I don't want to know or hear about that."

She grabbed my hand and squeezed it. "Dad even mentioned moving up his retirement date so we could do a trip across Europe."

"What would you do with Muppet?" I asked.

"Oh, Muppet would be taken care of. I'm sure I could find a pet sitter for the house."

"You've got plenty of time to plan," I assured her.

We walked back into the main room, where Maddie was already chopping away on celery, when I saw Nick making his way down the driveway.

A jolt of excitement spread through me as he walked up the steps and knocked on the door. This wasn't how a person should feel over a friend wandering over.

"Were you expecting someone?" my mom asked.

"No, but it looks like it's Nick."

"Oh, good. I can't thank him enough." My mom had a dopey grin on her face as I opened the door.

Nick looked sensational in a wool tweed sweater and slouchy, worn jeans. His brown eyes caught mine for a second before he glanced at my flannel pajamas that I forgot I was wearing and sheepishly tried to cover up.

"You're certainly a hit with my parents. I can't believe you did all that for them."

The smile grew, and he nodded. "I'm glad they enjoyed it. My friend specializes in theme cruises, and I thought a little romance was in order. I just wanted to drop by and make sure it all went okay."

"More than okay. It's like a magical fairy dust was sprinkled over my mom, and I couldn't imagine a better gift for Thanksgiving. So, what time are you headed to your friends' for turkey?"

"Sophie and Natty both caught the flu. They're still doing the whole thing, but I really don't feel like coming down with the plague, so I'm spending a nice, quiet evening in with a Cornish game hen. I thought you were going to your sister's?" He glanced at my dad and mom inside.

"Her pipes broke and her kitchen is a mess, so we're doing turkey day here. Why don't you join us?"

I felt my family's eyes on us and stared pleadingly at Nick. He looked over my shoulder and brought his gaze back to mine.

"Really?"

"I'd be forever in your debt," I told him.

"When you put it that way." A mischievous glint in his eyes made my stomach flutter. "Should I come back later, closer to dinner?"

"Nah. Now's as good a time as any." I grabbed his wrist and yanked him into my house without giving him any reason to back out.

"Nick, thanks for planning that cruise." My dad stood up from the table. "It was exactly what the doctor ordered."

"Dad's even talking about retiring a couple of months early." I grinned.

Nick looked completely at ease, and I swore I saw relief dash through him.

"That's great." Nick nodded, his eyes landing on the floral arrangement. "Where did you get this?"

"Natty did it. Custom order to suit my *mom's* taste." Maddie said, dotting each word, giving him fair warning.

"It's quite something," Nick said, nodding. "Spectacular. Definitely captures the spirit of the season."

My dad held in a chuckle as I went to help my sister in the kitchen.

"Do you ever think the world has an incredible way of working out?" my sister asked as my eyes welled up with tears from the onion.

I looked over my breakfast bar at Nick, who was talking to my father about woodworking, as my mom stared at them both with a silly look on her face. I'd never imagined our Thanksgiving to work out like this, but I was grateful for the man who seemed to make it happen.

Nick's eyes connected with mine, and I knew behaving around him was going to be extra tricky, but it was a necessity. He was a great guy and a loyal friend, but not boyfriend material, and I knew I'd fall for him hard because I already had.

Chapter Thirteen

It was the day after Thanksgiving, and I woke up with a pounding headache, stuffed-up nostrils, sore throat and nausea. I groaned into the cot and heard a hiss as the thin air mattress deflated with me still on it.

Wouldn't it figure?

I blinked open my eyes and noticed it wasn't even light out yet. I let out a huff and stretched my arms, but every muscle ached so I snuggled back under the covers on the wobbly cot.

My lips were all crusty from breathing out of my mouth all night, and I just felt like a wreck.

I was supposed to be to work at ten to prepare for Black Friday, but I couldn't imagine anyone being thrilled about me scooping tea leaves for them in my condition. A cough erupted from my lungs and I sat up, hacking my lungs out.

Ugh.

I hoisted myself off the floor and shivered from the chilly air. I made my way to the bathroom, brushed my teeth, loaded and lit the fireplace, and made myself a pot of coffee before sinking into my favorite chair.

Pulling a red chenille blanket around my shoulders, I sniffed in and then sneezed. I needed to let my sister know I wouldn't be in. I picked my phone up from the coffee table and texted a quick message, along with a photo of how wretched I looked for proof.

I took in a deep breath through my mouth and closed my eyes, feeling absolutely nothing from the caffeine as I drifted to sleep.

It wasn't until I heard a light tapping on the door that I woke up, feeling even worse than when I'd fallen asleep. It was light out, so I had no idea how long I'd slept. I hugged the blanket around my shoulders and peeked out the glass to see Nick standing on my porch.

My heart squeezed at the sight of him, but then I panicked. There was nothing cute about this look.

"You okay in there, Holly?" he asked through the door. "I saw your car in the driveway, but you said you worked today."

"Totally—" I started hacking before I got the rest of my sentence out.

"Open up." He sounded worried, and in between coughing fits, my heart melted even more for the man on the other side of the door, which told me that on the other side was where he needed to stay.

"I've just got a flu or cold or something." I spurted it out before another coughing fit.

"You must have gotten it from Sophie." He let out a groan. "Or Natty. You saw them both when they were contagious and didn't know it. It's a bad bug."

"I'm kind of guessing that."

"Do you have any medicine?" he asked.

I let out a sigh, followed by a sneeze.

"No."

"I'll go to the pharmacy and pick up some stuff. Is there anything in particular you want?" He was still talking to the door.

"Nick, you don't have to do that. I'll be fine."

He was making it really difficult not to like him even more, and I somewhat resented him for it. After all, he wasn't the settling-down kind. Now, I was completely capable of having a fling, but it was like Nick unknowingly wrapped himself in the perfect package that made me like the idea of something more with him. So really, it's his fault. I had to shut it down before it went somewhere. If he were shallow and inconsiderate, it would be way easier to imagine a casual fling or nothing at all.

"There's nothing worse than feeling sick and trying to go out to pick things up. Just promise me you'll open the door when I return."

"Fine," I grumbled and schlepped back to my chair.

I picked up my phone and saw several

messages from my sister, along with the time. It was noon? I'd slept that long in a chair?

Nick certainly knew how to build furniture.

I let out a sigh and grabbed the remote for the television. *Top Gun* was on, and it was at the good part, the part where they were playing volleyball.

This sick day was meant to be. I curled deeper into the chair and messaged my sister back with an update.

It didn't seem like very much time had passed at all when Nick knocked on the door. Another coughing fit led me to the door, and I felt bad for even exposing him to whatever this was.

"You can just leave it on the porch. I don't want you to catch this, whatever it is."

"Holly, I was at your house yesterday when you were the most contagious, so I'm probably already doomed." His laughter filled me with happiness, and I cursed myself for being such a girl and noticing.

"Fine," I huffed. "But I don't want you holding anything against me with what you're about to see."

I flung open the door, and Nick smirked.

"You're cute even when you're sick."

I rolled my eyes and invited him in.

"Don't say I didn't warn you. If you get sick—"

"I expect you to take care of me," he interrupted, stepping inside and glancing at the television. "I see your taste in movies is the same as music."

I laughed.

"I swear I have more interests." I felt the tickle in my chest and ushered him away as I started coughing into the crook of my arm.

Nick was already in the kitchen pulling out cough drops, flu medicine, and a bottle of something I didn't recognize.

"What in the world is that?" I asked, leaning against the dining room table.

"Rock and rye." He grinned. "It'll knock you on your ass, but it'll cure what ails you. At least, that's what the label says."

"Sounds like an old wives' tale." I grinned.

"Probably, but I bet it will make you sleep well."

"Then pour it up." My head started spinning, and I slid onto a dining chair. "Are Sophie and Natty doing better?"

Nick grimaced. "Worse, actually. That's how I knew to go get what I could now. I also got you some sports drinks."

"Why?" My brow arched.

"So you don't dehydrate." He brought over two glasses with the liquor in it.

"Is this just an excuse so you can have some?" I teased.

"Kind of." He grinned and took a sip, sucking in his cheeks. "Whoa."

"That's not exactly what I wanted to see." I smiled, noticing how I was already feeling better just having him around.

He tossed a pack of throat lozenges on the table and took another sip, prompting me to do the same.

The moment the liquid hit my lips, I wanted to spit it out, but I swallowed the first sip.

"That's strong."

"Should kill the virus quickly, no doubt." He took the last sip, and I took another gulp.

By the time I finished, I was feeling ready to go back to bed.

The credits were running on the movie, and I stretched, feeling the warmth of the liquor running through my veins . . . or maybe it was being around Nick.

"I think I'd better get to my chair to sleep." I spoke through a yawn.

"Don't you think a bed would be more comfortable, or at least, the couch?"

"I like the chair. Some sexy woodworker builds them on the island," I told him.

"Is that so?" he asked. "How sexy?"

"Too much so for his own good. He's not the type to settle down."

"Where'd you hear that?" His brows quirked up.

"Just something I know," I slurred.

"How about I help you into your bed, and you call me if you need anything?"

I shook my head. "My bed deflated."

"Of course it did." He shook his head. "Then that settles it. You're staying in my guest room until you shake this bug."

I took in a breath to object, but the coughing fit that took over only allowed me to surrender without protest.

"Thank you." I patted his shoulder. "You're a

wonderful neighbor to have."

"And so are you." The tone in his voice had lost the playfulness, but I was far too exhausted to say anything. "I know this seems crazy, but I'm gonna go get the truck."

"It doesn't seem silly at all," I said, collapsing my head on my hands.

"Okay, great." He put all the supplies back in the bag, poured a little more rye for me to swallow, and took off out the front door without waiting for me to change my mind.

But I felt too horrible to argue, and the idea of a deflated cot on the floor wasn't that appealing.

The rumble of Nick's truck alerted me to his quick return. He came back inside and helped me to the truck, got me settled, and went back inside to take care of locking up. When he climbed in the truck, I rolled my head over to look at him.

"Thank you." I touched his leg and he stiffened. Or maybe it was my imagination.

"Nothing to thank me for."

"Everything to thank you for." I shut my eyes as he reversed out of the driveway, across the road, and into his driveway. "That was fast." I giggled, which only turned into coughing as he slid out of the truck.

This was so not how I wanted to impress him. He helped me out of the truck and into his house filled with warmth and a set of stairs that looked like death in my condition. Without a word said, he scooped me into his arms and carried me up the stairs and into the guest room.

"Hope this is okay," he said, placing me gently

on the bed.

"More than," I said, shutting my eyes.

"Your mom's coming over to check on you. I called your sister and let her know I was moving you to my guest room from your deflated bed."

My eyes flashed open.

"Muppet's not coming over, I hope." I let out a labored breath.

"Bird-free zone," he promised. "Plus, we wouldn't want to get Muppet sick."

"God forbid." I grinned, feeling the softness of the comforter surrounding me.

"Here's the remote for the television. I'm sure there are some good eighties flicks On-Demand for you. I'll bring up some soup in a little bit."

I smiled.

"You would make a sensational boyfriend." I studied him, the rye confusing my senses. "It's a shame, really."

His lip curled up slightly. "Holler if you need anything."

I nodded as he left the guest room, and that was when I realized I wasn't the luckiest neighbor in the world. I was the unluckiest woman to ever move to Fireweed.

With that thought, I fell back asleep, only to hear my mom's voice in the room. I opened my eyes to see her talking to Nick in the corner of the room. At some point during my sleep, I must have stuffed tissue up my nose.

Great!

"Hey," I said, but another eruption happened and I started coughing.

This was definitely not the way to show a man how sexy I could be. There was no doubt about it. We were in the friend zone.

"You look horrible," my mom said, rushing to my side and sweeping some of my hair from my face.

"Thanks," I said sarcastically.

"Well, you're sick. You can't help it," she continued.

"Thanks again." I smiled and Nick came over.

"I think she looks cute." Nick glanced at my mom, and they traded some weird all-knowing glances while I sat with tissue stuck up my nose. "Want some more rye?"

"That sounds perfect."

He laughed.

"Just try to get some more sleep. If you need anything, Dad and I'll cancel our trip on the water that's tomorrow. You're more important."

"Love you," I said, smiling.

"Love you, too, Shortcake."

Nick's eyes flew to mine.

"I used to love Strawberry Shortcake," I answered without waiting for him to ask the question.

"Makes complete sense." A smile swept across his mouth.

"Get some rest. I can show myself out." My mom gave a quick wave and left Nick and me alone in the room.

"Feeling better or worse?" he asked.

"Worse, but better for being here."

"Good. That's what I wanted to hear. I made

some soup, but you fell asleep. Are you hungry?"

"Not really."

"Well, let me bring some up anyway."

I nodded, but before he left, I asked a question I really didn't want answered.

"Are you this nice to all your friends?"

"I hope so. Friends are hard to come by, and good friends are almost impossible, so if you find a good one . . ."

"You think you've found a good one?"

"I know I did." He ruffled my already messy hair, and I knew without a shadow of a doubt that I'd never get out of the friend zone. Maybe that was okay because I certainly wouldn't want to lose a friend like this over a lusty fling that jeopardized anything.

Chapter Fourteen

Five days later, I was starting to feel human again. Today was my first day back at the shop. My sister was taking today and tomorrow off, which was more than well-deserved since I'd been out of commission for the last few days. It had been a busy Tuesday, which made it go quickly. I was surprised to see the sun had already set, and several customers were busy sniffing teas and bringing tins to the counter.

I never had days go by so fast at my old job. The minutes usually felt like hours.

It had been a good day and a great several days. I had my head back on straight. I knew what I had with Nick and Fireweed was a good thing. I didn't want to lose the sensational feeling of both, so keeping Nick in the friendship bucket was the smartest thing to do.

"Do you think the spicy hot chocolate is too much for Grandma?" A little girl asked her mom.

"No. I think it'll give her the kick she needs." The mom turned to look at me. "It's not too spicy, is it?"

I shook my head. "Just a hint."

"Perfect."

As they trundled up to the cash register, I saw Nick walk by the window, slowing to admire the twinkle lights we'd just put up. I gave a slight wave, and the woman followed my gaze.

"Well, he's delicious." She laughed, and I glanced down at her ring finger. She wasn't wearing one.

"Yes, he is, and he's single." I grinned, ringing her up.

I figured the more practice I had with not caring about Nick dating around, the better off I'd be. All of his other best friends seem to manage just fine, so I needed to be one of them.

"Well, maybe I'll have to bump into him before we leave the island." She laughed and glanced down at her daughter. "Hope he likes kids."

"Well, he likes birds, so I'm sure kids are fine."

She gave me a puzzled look as I packaged her items, and I wanted to kick myself.

This not caring thing was unpleasant.

"Have a nice day," I told her as she hurried out the door with her sack of tea and her daughter.

She accidentally bumped right into Nick, and I did a phenomenal job of not caring as she giggled in front of him, flipping her hair and batting her

161

lashes.

Nick glanced in my direction, and I immediately dropped my gaze to the counter, pretending to organize the pen jar.

A woman brought over two canisters of tea and placed them on the counter.

"An ounce of each, please." She smiled. "Maddie's not in today?"

"No. She's taking today and tomorrow off. Did you want me to give her a message?" I asked.

The woman shook her head. "Not at all. Just thought it would be nice to bump into her and fill her in on my son. I live on Hound."

"Your son?" I asked. "Are you Hildie?"

She nodded. "That's me."

"So good to meet you. I'm Maddie's sister, Holly."

Hildie was the owner of the lavender farm. I'd only spoken with her over the phone, but she matched my imagination's version of her perfectly with sparkling blue eyes and silver streaks running through her dark hair.

"I thought you looked like Maddie." She beamed. "You're both such pretty girls."

"Yes, they are," Nick said, coming into the store.

My cheeks blushed as I continued scooping the teas.

"Nick, you are ever the opportunist." Hildie chuckled, and I immediately relaxed.

"Yes, he is." I looked up at Nick, and my heart dropped to my toes.

Spending sick days with him only made him

more appealing. Who was I kidding about being able to dump him into the friend zone?

"So you've heard about him all the way over on Hound Island?" I laughed, shaking my head. "Sounds about right."

"I think it's mostly rumor. He's got a reputation to uphold." She winked. "But actually, my son is engaged to Jewels."

"Really? I had no idea."

"My son is Jake."

"The fireman?" I asked, and Nick's brows rumpled.

Hildie chuckled. "That's him."

"What a small world." I swiped her card and handed her the bag.

She took in a deep breath. "I can't tell you how nice it is to get some tea without the purple stuff."

"Hildie, don't let that get out," Nick teased. "That purple stuff is your livelihood."

"Lovesick looks good on you." She tapped his cheek with her thumb.

"I'm not—"

"Oh, I must have been mistaken," she interrupted him, grinning. She flashed a look in my direction. "Anyway, don't forget to come visit the farm and bring your sister."

"We can't wait. The shop is closed on Mondays, so that might be the best day."

"All days work for me." She held up her bag. "Have a great evening. I'd better go try to catch the last ferry, or I'll be barging in on Jake and Jewels again."

"I'm sure they don't mind." Nick laughed as Hildie exited.

The store was now empty, and the energy immediately changed.

"So what brings you here, stranger?" I asked.

"Just had a few errands to run."

"I see one of our customers was excited to bump into you." I wiggled my brows and adjusted my ponytail.

"Why do I think you sent her outside to greet me?" He shoved his hands into his jean pockets.

"I'd never do that." I turned off the computer. "But she does meet your qualifications. She's not from Fireweed."

"True. That's definitely a positive." He pushed his hands deeper into his pockets. "How are you feeling?"

"Ninety-nine-point-nine percent better."

"So good enough to let me take you somewhere?" he asked.

"Where's somewhere?" I turned off the lights in the back room and reappeared without my apron.

"Christmas tree farm."

"At night?" I asked.

"Best time to go. They have lights."

"Well, I do need a tree." I nodded, grabbing my purse. "And it would be nice to have a second opinion. It is a big decision, after all."

"Perfect. I'll drive." A devilish grin appeared, and the familiar flutter uprooted me.

"So did you get that woman's number?" I asked.

"I haven't gotten numbers in a long time."

I shot him a look of surprise. "How about texts, messages, swipes?" I chuckled.

A dimple surfaced in his left cheek.

"You have dimples," I gushed. "How cute."

"I have one, and very few people can get it out of me."

"Boy, you do know what to say." I shook my head, glancing down to see his boots. "All right, cowboy, let's get this show on the road."

His laughter boomed through the air as I shut off the shop lights.

"I was helping my buddy with his horses today." He followed me outside.

"So you have an outfit for every occasion?" I teased.

"You're obviously feeling better."

"I told you I'm only a tenth of a percent away from perfection." I beamed, trying to ignore how aware of Nick I was. It was like I could feel him even a foot away.

"You're right about that." Nick slid his arm around my waist, leading us toward his truck, and the rush of being so close to him threw me off course. Or maybe it was his words.

The tree farm was only a fifteen-minute drive. It was actually near our homes, but down the main road a few more miles.

"Do you ever wonder why our road is a state road? It sounds so technical. Where's the romance? We need it changed to Birchwood Avenue or something." I grinned, tapping my finger to the music playing.

He glanced at me out of the corner of his eye, and I swore his smile grew wider.

"What?" I asked as he turned down a gravel road.

"Your mind. I like how it works."

"Okay." I furrowed my brows.

He parked next to another pickup, and I had to say, for being a tree farm, the place was really well-lit.

"Ready?" he asked, hopping out of the truck.

"For sure." I climbed out of the truck and glanced at the small shed in front of us. "This place is super cute."

"It's the only place to get a tree." He grabbed my hand and pulled me toward the small building.

Green garlands wrapped each of the two windows and entrance. An outdoor snowman stood waving, and several automated penguins skated behind. Nick switched from holding my hand to wrapping his arm around my waist.

"Before we head out to find your perfect tree, we need to sign in and grab our hot chocolates and saw." He led me into the office, where a tray of peppermint brownies sat.

"Hey, Floyd. How's it going?" Nick asked the older gentleman seated behind a desk.

"Back already?" Floyd asked, glancing at me before turning to stare at Nick.

My stomach tightened. Had Nick already brought someone else here?

"This time it's not for my house, but for Holly's."

Floyd stood up. "Any friend of Nick's is a friend of mine."

"Nice to meet you." I shook his hand.

Nick let go of me and wandered over to the wall of saws.

"Feel free to grab some hot chocolate and a brownie." Floyd smiled. "My wife makes them every morning."

"Thank you." I grinned, turning to the table to make the hot cocoa and snatch a brownie.

I wrapped up two brownies in a napkin and held our drinks as we wandered out the door and toward the acres of Christmas trees. Nick took his drink in his free hand and took a sip.

"So how long have you been coming here?" I asked.

"Forever."

I took a nibble of the brownie. "Wow. These are incredible."

"Here, let me have a little taste." He glanced down at me, and I held up my brownie since he didn't have a free hand.

He took a bite and groaned. "So good."

"This is really why you brought me here, isn't it? You were just craving brownies."

He stopped abruptly, and I almost crashed into him.

"Now this is a sensational tree." He took a step back, admiring the fluffy Douglas fir.

"It is pretty fabulous, but what if there's another one even better?"

He scowled. "I don't know. This one's pretty good."

"But we've barely scratched the surface. There are thousands of trees in front of us."

"But this tree is beautiful. It's a perfect fit for the space."

"There's no doubt about that." I twisted my lips as I bounced the branches with the back of my hand. "I just think we need to keep searching. We can come back to this one."

"What if someone else snags it?" he asked.

"Then it wasn't meant to be."

"Why risk it?"

"I like to live on the edge." I grinned.

"Do you really?" He motioned for another bite of brownie.

"Sometimes. At least when it comes to Christmas trees."

"All right, let's keep going, but we'll come back to this one. Guarantee it."

"Fine. Wanna bet on it?" I asked.

He shrugged. "Sure."

"Okay, if we don't find a more perfect tree for my cabin, I'll make you a basketful of Christmas cookies."

"And if we do find a better one?" he asked.

"How about you have to endure a night of eighties movies?"

He laughed as I polished off the first brownie, readying to unwrap the second.

"Deal."

"Speaking of which, you still haven't had a pickle and peanut butter sandwich."

"Had one this morning. It's my new breakfast food."

"It is not." We began hiking through the maze of trees, spotting lots of great ones, but none quite as good as the first.

"See what happens when you think the grass is greener?" he teased.

"I don't think the grass is greener." I stopped and turned to face him. "I just don't want to miss out."

He watched me as the revelation slowly developed.

"I've got another bet for us." He tossed the saw on the ground.

"Lay it on me."

Nick took a step closer and my pulse spiked.

"If we're both still single on New Year's Eve, how about we take a trip together—" He stopped himself.

"Ha." I laughed, catching his gaze. "To where?"

"Do you ski?" he asked.

"I can make it down a hill." I nodded.

"Then I've got the perfect place."

"You're so strange." I studied him. "I can't tell what it is you want out of this." I motioned between us. "And how is that even a bet?"

He shook his head. "Maybe it's not."

"Maybe it's just a way to make sure you have a date for the second most dateless night of the year." My brow arched.

"That's exactly what it is," he agreed.

"You know what, buddy? I'm gonna call you on your bull." I tapped my foot against some dried pine needles. "If you're still single and I'm still single, you're stuck with me."

"This bet sealed with a kiss instead of a handshake?" he asked, seeming unfazed by this life-changing agreement.

"Is that what you want?" I felt a tidal wave between my ears as my blood rushed through my head. I felt lightheaded, but I wanted nothing more than to be kissed by Nick.

He closed the gap between us, and with his free hand, his finger combed through my hair, bringing me closer as I looked up into his eyes.

"What are you doing?" I asked.

"Something I should've done a long time ago." His voice lowered. "You're irresistible, and Lord knows I've tried to resist."

"Have you?" I whispered before his lips sank to mine.

The electricity traveling through my body as I slipped my free arm around his waist, feeling his body next to mine, was thrilling.

I parted my lips, feeling his tongue push deeper, and I could barely stay upright. It was like all the flirting and kindness had finally exploded into a tangled knot of emotions of want and need.

Everything about the way he moved his hand through my hair, the deliberate stroke of his tongue, and his ragged breathing was sexually charged with the same longing I'd been holding onto.

I tore my lips away, barely able to breathe, wishing there was a place to continue, but my heart was racing so quickly, I needed a second. I was afraid.

Afraid I wouldn't be able to turn back to our friendship if things went wrong.

I looked into Nick's eyes, and my heart felt like it was going to shatter. I didn't understand the emotions running through his gaze. Were they matching my worries?

Was it regret, longing, need? What was it?

He skimmed his thumb across my cheek and brought his lips back down to mine, sending my worries far away as the warmth of his mouth made my world spin.

Nick let out a low and sexy growl, and my entire world stood still. His mouth moved from mine, his lips hovering so close.

"You taste so good," he whispered, his other hand threading through my hair as I felt his hardness against me. I dropped my paper cup and teased my fingers along his back, feeling the warmth of his skin under my fingertips.

His mouth fastened back on mine, and every nerve in my body was tingling in anticipation as our kisses deepened. I'd wanted this man from the moment I saw him, and now I was getting a taste.

Nick's breathing changed and his kisses slowed, even though my pulse quickened as I opened my eyes.

"You're the sweetest thing I've ever come across," he whispered, his eyes dazed with longing.

"Nick . . ." I took a breath. "I'm scared that we'll never get this back. The before, I mean."

His eyes flicked a shade darker, and I

swallowed the strange feeling of longing and remorse tied into one big mess. Everything I wanted with Nick tore me in opposite directions. I wanted our friendship to stay the same, but I wanted more from him, something more that he might not be able to give me, and I refused to let that jeopardize our friendship.

Nick brought me into him, and I pressed my head against his chest, hearing his quickened heart rate.

"I'm sorry," I whispered.

"You have nothing to be sorry for," he said softly, still holding me.

Tears pricked my eyes, and I wondered if I'd just thrown away the best thing that could have been.

Chapter Fifteen

My sister and I were with Sophie in Seattle for some Christmas shopping. I hadn't told a soul about the kiss or the not-quite bet, but that didn't mean both thoughts didn't invade just about every vacant moment.

Nick's lips had to be the softest I'd ever experienced, and his technique?

It made me weak in the knees just thinking about it, and to spend New Year's with him?

Even better, but I was confused beyond belief for several reasons.

The top reason being that I hadn't heard from him since. Five days, six if you count today, had gone by, and nothing—not a text, phone call, or drop-in. It was like he was working overtime to ensure he spent the holiday with someone else.

Now I was left to deal with the aftermath of

the accidental kiss. At the time, I didn't think it was accidental, but now I was positive.

While he was able to go on his merry way, I was daydreaming about how amazing that kiss was.

It didn't help that Nick's truck hadn't been at his house the last three days. Maybe downtown Seattle was treating him too well.

I grunted.

"Were you even listening?" Maddie asked, holding up a pair of earrings.

"Quite possibly not," I said sheepishly.

"I said, do you think Mom would like these?"

I stared at the simple gold earrings. They were pretty, but Mom usually liked a little more oomph.

"Boy, you really weren't listening." My sister sighed. "You buy these charms for the earrings. Isn't it a cute idea?"

Maddie held up a pair of ruby red charms that were meant to dangle from the gold earrings in the other hand. I fully saw Mom written all over them.

"Perfect." I glanced around, not seeing Sophie.

"What's gotten into you lately?" Maddie asked.

I couldn't tell her.

"Just wondering what I want to do with my life. No big deal." I grinned and saw a scarf my mom would love. I motioned for the sales associate, who helped get it out of the case.

"That's always good to do right before the holidays." She giggled.

"Isn't it though? Where'd Sophie go?" I asked

as we paid for our items.

"The bookstore across the street. We're going to meet her at the coffee shop inside."

"Awesome." I decided to purchase the scarf and took my bag from the clerk. "It's nice to have Mondays off so we can hang out together without tea surrounding us."

"It's a nice change." She took her bag after paying for the earrings, and we wandered outside, feeling the crisp air alert us to another change in the weather.

"Do you think we'll really get snow again?" I asked as we waited for the crosswalk.

The sun was setting, and the Christmas lights up and down the Seattle streets were turning on, store by store.

"Possibly. I hope so."

By the time we got back inside, my fingers were icicles and I was never happier to see a place that served warm drinks.

Sophie waved at us as we quickly got our drinks and made our way over to the table by the window overlooking the busy sidewalks.

"Get everything you wanted?" Maddie asked.

"I did." She lifted her bookstore bag. "How about you guys?"

"Earrings and a scarf for our mom. Getting closer to being done." Maddie slid into the seat next to Sophie.

I took the chair across from both and sat with a thud.

"How are you enjoying your family room?" Sophie asked.

"Love it. Can't get enough of it." I smiled. "Thank you so much for all your help on it. I could never have pulled it off."

"You picked it all out," Sophie said.

"From a store I couldn't go wrong in." I grinned, sighing. "I got my tree up and everything. I couldn't ask for a better place to call home."

"I know." Sophie wiggled her nose. "I heard about the Christmas tree. Isn't that a great little place?"

I glanced at my sister, feeling my cheeks flush.

"What?" Maddie asked.

"Nothing," I said quickly.

Sophie giggled.

"Sophie, now you *have* to tell me." Maddie smacked her.

"Nick kissed Holly at the Christmas tree farm." Sophie's eyes twinkled with delight.

"Are there no secrets on Fireweed?" I said, exasperated.

"Not many." Sophie's smile only widened.

"And you didn't tell me?" My sister's eyes were huge.

I let out a deep sigh. "There's nothing to tell. I haven't heard from him since."

Sophie's gaze dropped to her latte.

"I'm sorry, Shortcake." Maddie twisted her lips into a pout. She only used that when she knew I felt like crap, and you know what? She was right. I felt like crap for breaking my own rules and thinking he'd break his.

"It's no big deal. I'd been warned about him.

It's my own fault," I assured her. "But he gives such mixed signals. One minute, he only dates people from Seattle, and the next, he's treating me to an amazing dinner and a hot tub, and the next thing I know, he has a harem of female best friends he tosses me into." I looked over at Sophie. "No offense."

She laughed. "None taken."

"I'm totally cool about it. I'd rather have his friendship than nothing at all. He's a handy guy to have living across the street." I looked at Sophie. "I'm sure that's how you felt too?"

Sophie shuddered. "Nick has never been more than a friend."

My sister even looked at her sideways.

Sophie threw both hands in the air. "I swear to God. I've never been with him, thought about him, been kissed by him . . . ever. It would be way too weird."

"So you're telling me you've never been attracted to Nick, even in the slightest?" Maddie asked, almost more stunned than I was.

"Swear on my life. He's always been a friend. Same with Tori and Natty. I know for a fact they've never been attracted to him." Sophie's eyes connected with mine. "Don't get me wrong. He's hot, but I just never thought of him as anything but a sweet and loyal friend. I understand why women trip over themselves to get to him, but he's just never done it for me."

I wondered how many women we were talking, considering I was staring at a woman who was with a rock star. It was all relative.

"So you set your boundaries, and he respected them," I prompted, trying a different approach at gaining the same information.

Sophie shook her head emphatically.

"No. I didn't have to set boundaries because he was never interested. Same with Natty and Tori. This is a two-way street. No interest from any party. Ever."

"In all the years you guys have known him, he's never tried to kiss any of you?" I didn't buy it.

"God, no." Sophie looked toward the ceiling and smiled. "I wonder if I should be offended."

I giggled, feeling as light as air.

For no reason.

It wasn't like Nick had suddenly called.

"Definitely." Maddie laughed.

"I just wish I didn't feel such a connection." I glanced out the window and saw the wind picking up and swirling around a few dried leaves that never got swept up by the street sweeper. "But I can ignore it." I nodded, reassuring myself. "Not to gross you out, but that man knows how to kiss."

Sophie snorted, and I realized Nick had really good taste when it came to friends.

"Since you're his friend, and I'm obviously in his friend category, what's your advice?" I asked Sophie. "How do I proceed to make sure I don't ruin the friendship?"

"But you said you feel a connection," Sophie said slowly, looking suddenly uncomfortable.

"Yeah, but that doesn't matter. It's got to be

both sides, and it obviously isn't."

"I wouldn't be so sure about that." Sophie slammed her mouth shut and looked extremely guilty.

"What are you getting at?" Maddie asked as my insides turned into a nervous mess of emotion.

Sophie groaned. "He will kill me. I can't say."

"You think *he'll* kill you?" My brows shot up, and I flexed my puny arms. "You can't leave me hanging."

Maddie and Sophie laughed.

"He's—" She shook her head. "I can't."

I felt my pulse swimming between my ears.

"Please. I'll give you free tea for life."

Maddie scowled at me. "Hey."

"Add it to my tab." I glanced at my sister.

"Nick hasn't had one Tinder date since he met you." She chewed on her lip. "He deleted his account." Her eyes met mine, and she pressed her lips together, looking completely tormented.

This was huge news.

That might mean absolutely nothing.

Or positively everything.

"He deleted his account?" I repeated, and she nodded.

"He'll kill me if he finds out I told you." She let out a huge sigh. "But it feels so much better getting it off my chest. He's had that stupid account since Tinder came into existence, I swear."

"Does that mean he's seeing someone from the account, maybe?" My sister asked cautiously.

"Nope." Sophie's gaze rested on mine. "Someone's caught his eye, and he's completely stumped."

"About what?" I asked, confused.

"He thinks you won't be able to get past his reputation, which is probably pretty inflated, truth be told." She leaned closer to the table. "He thinks you've been sending clear friend-zone signals."

"I don't kiss my friends that way," I whispered.

"I don't either." Sophie giggled. "But I think you've turned his world upside down. Half the time he talks to me, it's about how much he can't stop thinking about you, and the other half, it's about how he has to forget about you because you're just not interested."

"But—" I clamped my mouth shut, allowing her words to sink in. I wanted to be excited, but I felt like there was a big *but* with this entire equation.

"What?" she asked.

"If he's interested, why hasn't he reached out since helping me with my Christmas tree?"

"That I can't answer." Sophie folded her arms across her chest. "I honestly don't know what's up. He kind of went off the radar."

"He's not at his house," I confirmed, but then panic struck. "Is he okay? Could something have happened?"

Sophie was too quick to shake her head. "No, he's fine. He just . . ." She shook her head. "I hate this. I'm just not good at keeping secrets."

"Secrets?" I asked.

Sophie groaned. "He's visiting his dad."

"Oh, well that doesn't seem abnormal." I watched Sophie squirm.

"They've been estranged since his parents' divorce," she added.

"Oh."

"Please don't tell him I told you."

"Not a word," I promised, unsure of the significance.

"I'm not trying to be Nick's cheerleader, but he is going to make some lucky lady very happy someday. Or at least, that's my hope for him. He's got a lot of hang-ups when it comes to relationships." She cocked her head. "Obviously."

"Yeah, well I doubt I've made it any easier on him." I smiled, running circles with my finger. "I've tried to make it really clear that I value our friendship, but I think I've made it too clear."

Sophie shrugged. "I'm trying to let you two run your course. I don't want to influence it whatsoever. Just because I know what I'd like to see happen, it doesn't mean that's what's best."

"I appreciate your honesty." I glanced at my sister, who nodded.

"In other news, I've got a cookie exchange coming up on Friday night. You guys game?" Sophie asked.

"I'm totally in," I agreed, thinking how quickly my entire world had changed by moving to Fireweed.

"Me too." My sister sounded equally excited.

"Awesome. Just bring your favorite cookies,

and adult beverages will be provided."

"Sounds like my kind of Friday night." I glanced outside, noticing the sudden change in the weather. "It's snowing."

Sophie shot up from the table. "That's our cue to get the heck out of Seattle. The ferries are going to be a mess."

We all grabbed our bags and headed outside, but all I could think about was Nick.

He never mentioned he deleted his Tinder account. I hadn't really seen him out and about much since I'd moved in, and regardless of what people said about him, he looked like he enjoyed spending most of his time at home. Maybe it was time I quit worrying about losing his friendship and see where this thing goes.

By the time Maddie pulled her car in the ferry line to head back to Fireweed, I was consumed with the idea of letting him know I wanted to experiment. I wasn't trying to tempt love. I just wanted to have a little fun.

A flutter of nervous excitement was quickly squashed the moment the text came over from Nick.

Can we talk? There's some stuff I've got to get off my chest.

I didn't answer. Instead, I shoved my cell back in my purse and waited for the ferry to get me back home to Fireweed.

Chapter Sixteen

I pulled in my driveway, and Nick was sitting on the steps. Snow was already covering the ground.

He had to be freezing. I wondered what on earth had possessed him to wait for me to show up. Although, he was dressed in a goose down jacket, so maybe he wasn't as cold as I thought.

By the time I reached the porch, he'd unzipped his jacket, removed his hood, and had the biggest smile on his face. I hadn't texted him back, and I refused to let Sophie's words influence me. Hearsay wasn't the best way to start or end a relationship, and I had no idea which path we were headed down.

"Where've you been, kissing bandit?" I asked, marching up the steps.

I needed to keep things playful.

"Doing some thinking." His smile lessened.

"Did it hurt?" I asked, and he shook his head.

A small laugh erupted.

"It does now," he said, patting his chest.

"You want to come inside?" I asked.

"Did you get my text?" he asked, not answering my question.

"I did." I nodded. "But I wanted to keep you on your toes."

"Your plan almost worked except I don't have any toes left. It's like twenty degrees outside."

I giggled.

"Serves you right for not texting me back since the Christmas tree outing."

"I was out of town."

"Since when do cellphones have such limited coverage?" I raised my brow, and a huge smile swept over his lips.

"Never one to go easy on me."

"Would you want me to?" I winked at him, slid the key in my lock, and pushed open the door.

It felt good to be home.

"So you said you had some stuff you had to get off your chest?" I asked, loading the fireplace. I'd become a master at warming my house and not burning it down, which I'd say was a real plus. "Did I do something wrong?"

"No. I don't think you ever could." He closed the door and took off his coat. I liked how he just made himself at home. Granted, he played a big part in getting the place to feel like a home, but it was nice.

He walked over to the chair and sat down. I

watched him carefully, my pulse starting to climb as I waited for him to say something, but he didn't.

"Would you like anything to drink? I can make some coffee to warm you up or—"

"I'm fine." He shook his head and sank deeper into the chair.

"I have to confess that your text kind of freaked me out. Is everything okay?" I asked.

He let out a sigh, which only worried me.

"I want to know what you're afraid of." It wasn't really a question.

"Afraid of?" I repeated, shocked this had turned to me.

I didn't really think of myself as afraid of anything. I didn't even have a security system. I mean, I locked my doors at night, but that was about as far as I took it.

I curled up on the couch and brought my eyes to his.

"I don't think I'm afraid of much." I glanced around my cabin. "Maybe it helps to have a buff neighbor across the street."

Nick laughed. "That's not exactly what I meant."

"After living in New York, there's not much to be afraid of out here. Well, I did about pass out when a bunny darted in front of me at like midnight, but I—"

"I'm talking about with us," he interrupted.

"With us?" I scowled.

"What about us makes you afraid of being with me?"

His question rocked my world. I wasn't expecting it. I was the one who asked questions, especially ones like this.

But he didn't let up. He leaned forward, propped his elbows on his knees, his eyes staying on mine, and waited for an answer.

"I didn't really think I was afraid of anything." I swallowed down my embarrassment. It wasn't like I wanted to be so inept at this discussion thing, but he turned the tables.

"I think you are. I think you're terrified of something, and that's why we'll always be friends." His eyes stayed on mine. "Always friends."

"Oh." I felt myself sucking on my lip and stopped immediately, glancing toward the floor.

This wasn't what I expected. I thought we were going to unpack the real issues with Nick.

"If you don't call it fear, what do you see it as?" he asked. "Why do you think you're so afraid of moving to the next level?"

A few seconds of silence sat between us. I was torn. I didn't know what to say. I never thought of myself as being afraid of anything . . . cautious, maybe.

"I guess I want to know if there's anything I can do to help," he tried again.

"Help?"

He nodded. "How can I get you to take a chance on me?"

Nick's words gutted me.

"Take a chance on you?" I asked.

"Yeah." He sat back in the chair, kicked out his

legs, and stretched his arms behind his head.

"So this is about us?"

"Most definitely about us." He bit his lip before blowing out a mock sigh. "Are you afraid I'll hurt you?"

I shook my head, the realization slowly dawning on me that he was right.

I was afraid. I was deeply afraid of losing an amazing friendship. I'd experienced so few genuine friendships that now that I had one, I'd do anything to preserve it. Even if that meant denying myself true happiness.

"I can tell something popped into that brain of yours," he said.

I could hear the smile in his voice, and all it did was tear me up inside.

"You know what scares me?" I brought my gaze to his. "That you know me better than I know myself."

"I doubt that's possible."

"I know it's possible." I walked over to the fireplace to rid myself of the chill that had suddenly surfaced. "I *am* afraid. I'm afraid of losing the most genuine friendship I've ever had in my life. The reason I did so well in New York was because I didn't have to deal with anything that I didn't want to. I knew the relationships I had were based on superficial connections. If I got sick, I had to get my own cold medicine and sleep on a lumpy bed. No one cared, and I was fine with that. Here, someone cares, and if I screw that up . . ." my voice trailed off.

"I'll always care about you," Nick said,

standing up.

I hugged myself, completely confused by the turn of events. This was supposed to be about him, and somehow, the huge spotlight had been turned on me.

"I like our friendship, Nick. I don't want it to go away, because I've never had one like it. Ever."

He walked over to me, and I closed my eyes, holding the tears in.

"For the record, no one wants to be sick on a deflated camping mat." Nick smiled. "So I'll always try to make sure that doesn't happen."

Damn him. How did he get this out of me?

"Thank you."

"I get it, though." He scooped me into his arms and held me tightly. "I really do. If this friendship represents that much . . ."

"I'd planned on telling you that I wanted to do the friends with benefits thing." I sniffled and his body rocked from laughter. "Seriously, I made up my mind on the ferry."

"That figures." He laughed, and I looked into his eyes, seeing the same kindness I'd seen so often. "Such is my luck."

"You're a really lucky guy," I told him. "You've got so many solid relationships."

"But I don't have the one that counts." He took a step back. "At least, not yet."

The way he was looking at me made my heart squeeze with joy and fear. I didn't want to ruin my one chance at happiness, but I also didn't want to destroy our friendship.

I sucked in a ragged breath and wiped my nose.

"Or maybe we should just get it out of our system. Enjoy a holiday fling. We could do it one time and not make it complicated." I took a deep breath, and Nick's eyes moved to my mouth.

"Don't tempt me," he interrupted.

"Unless you're not interested," I added, taking a step back.

"Oh, I'm interested, but I'm a nice guy." He grinned. "It's a condition."

"You know what I think?"

"I honestly don't have a clue." He chuckled.

"I think you might like the idea of me, and I might let you down once you get me. It's not every day a guy meets a girl dancing in her bra. Perhaps I'm not all I'm cracked up to be," I joked. "This could be a way of saving yourself from complete and utter disappointment."

Nick's gaze fastened on mine, and the pull to him shook me to my core.

"We have a problem," he told me in a low voice.

"What's the problem?"

"I can't *just* be friends with you." He glanced toward his house. "I'm stuck between a rock and a hard spot."

My eyes fell to his package.

"Not literally." He laughed, throwing his head back.

"See? This is what gets me. I can't stop thinking about you, Holly. You make me laugh. You make my days brighter. You bring joy to my life in every possible way. Do you realize I was happy you got sick so I had the chance to take care of you and spend more time with you?" He stepped closer and moved his finger along my cheek. "The difference is that I know there is something here worth the risk. I'm just going to have to wait until you figure that out."

I swallowed hard and kept my eyes steadied on his.

"I'm a quick learner," I whispered. "Maybe one kiss wouldn't hurt. It could be like homework and then I could move on to the more challenging tasks."

"You make it extremely difficult to do what's right in a situation like this," Nick said, running his fingers along his jaw.

He licked his lips, and I couldn't take my eyes away from his mouth. A cloud hovered over his expression, but I felt the restraint slipping away from both of us.

"Just one kiss," I murmured.

Nick brought his mouth down to mine, and I lost myself in his arms. We poured everything we had into this kiss. I could feel the conflict, the desire, and the raw need as he pulled me into him. Every part of me wanted to spend the night with him. I wanted to experience all of him. All the emotions crashing inside me only made that sensation more intense, and I cursed myself for ever revealing what was behind my worries. Lust was taking over every active brain cell, and I was okay with that.

Everything I'd been feeling the last month was

manifesting in this one kiss. I didn't want it to end, but I knew it would.

I let out a moan, and his mouth slowly parted from mine as if that was his cue that it had gone on too long.

"You don't have to stop," I told him. Every part of my body was on fire and wanting more.

"I do." He nodded. "This can't be rushed. It's too important."

"One more kiss?"

He smirked but saw right through me. There was very little chance either of us would be able to stop.

But I didn't care. His lips hovered less than an inch from mine. It wouldn't take much for another.

Maybe reverse psychology would work.

"You know, you're right. I didn't think this through. Now's not the time," I whispered.

A flash of confusion shot through his gaze.

"I still don't have a bed," I continued.

With hooded lids, he swept a kiss across my lips, and my breath hitched in surprise.

"That's okay," he murmured between kisses, pulling me tight against him. "You have a chair, a couch, a counter, a wall."

"All those places?" I asked as my breathing quickened.

"That's only the beginning," he promised.

A shiver rolled over me, imagining each scenario as he kissed me harder, looping his arms around my waist.

"Holly," he said in a low and needy voice.

"Yeah?" my voice was hijacked from the intensity of the moment.

"Friends with benefits won't work." His hands skimmed under my sweater and along my bare belly. "But you already know that."

He kissed me one last time, and I felt his firmness pressing into me. It took everything I had not to beg him for more as his mouth slowly left mine still tingling.

"I don't want to hurt you. It would kill me to be the one to make you doubt your decisions for any reason at all." He shook his head.

"I take back everything I said earlier." I smiled. "It was a weak moment. I have lots of friends. You're one of many, and I want to see where this goes."

"Don't rush it. I'll be here waiting as your friend. Whatever else might come our way will come when it's meant to." He smiled.

I let out a long breath. "I can't believe you're going to leave me hanging like this."

"You're the one with the neck massager." His smile widened.

"You like that visual, don't you?" I teased.

"I'm not confirming or denying." He grabbed his jacket and headed out the door while I was left wondering what I'd gotten myself into.

Chapter Seventeen

I texted Nick a couple of times, and he returned the favor over the last couple of days. He was polite, but there wasn't any flirting. I saw him a few times when I drove into my driveway or got the mail.

He brought over a huge poinsettia.

You read that right.

I took it as a sign that he was trying to progress as friends without adding any extra pressure.

Regardless, I was going to take very good care of the red speckled plant.

I wrapped plastic wrap over my platter of cookies for tomorrow and let out a sigh. The problem appeared to be that confessing my revelation to him made me feel like he was being more guarded. It probably wasn't on purpose, but that was how it felt. I didn't want things to stall. I wanted them to progress.

Not only that, but I was certain he was a master at turning around situations. When I arrived back at my house last night, I thought he was going to be the one opening up to me. After all, he was the one with the revolving door of women. Yet somehow, he got me to reveal some deep secret that I'd been hiding in my subconscious while he got to waltz out my door unscathed.

Without one single reveal.

I glanced out the window and saw his truck in the driveway. The snow from the other night had completely melted and the temperature had risen to the forties, but I still bundled up for the short walk. I had about an hour before I had to be to the tea shop, which should be plenty of time to hear what he'd been up to.

As I got closer, I saw the light on in the workshop and heard a saw. I stopped, wondering if I should turn around. I didn't want to interrupt.

Well, I kind of did. I craned my neck to see through one of the windows.

Nick looked so incredibly in control as he guided the router along the wood, and I groaned at how turned on he made me. It was nice of him to expose what my hang-ups were about dating him, but it was time I got over them.

I walked over to the door and waited for him to turn off the tool before I knocked. It sounded like it only took him a few steps before he got to the door.

"Who is it?" he asked.

"Holly." I didn't even finish before he swung open the door.

"I hope it's okay that I stopped by," I said, peeking through the door.

"Absolutely." He seemed genuinely happy.

"Is that a hammer in your pocket or are you just happy to see me?" I asked.

"You didn't just say that."

"I believe I did." I laughed and shook my head. "I've always wanted to see what goes on over here."

"Is that so?" he folded his arms and took a step back, letting me inside his workshop.

"It's a regular Santa's Workshop inside here."

"They don't call me Jolly Old Saint Nick for nothing." He laughed and I spun around.

"They do?"

"No, but it seemed fitting."

"Wow. This is gorgeous." I ran my hand along the grain of the wood. It looked like the beginning of a sleigh bed. Intricate scrollwork ran throughout the pieces. Nick's style was impossible to miss.

"You like it?" he asked.

"Love it." I shook my head. "You're so talented."

"Just a lot of practice." He slowly walked over to me, and I felt my body already responding to his.

"I still have to go over to the Loxxy. That's what the hotel is called, right? Sophie mentioned that a lot of the pieces over there are yours. I want to see them."

He nodded. "Yeah. That was one of my first large orders."

"So I wanted you to know the poinsettia is doing really well."

"Good. I've been worried about it." A hidden smile coated his expression. "I never asked. Are you going to check out the polar bear dip?"

"What is that?" I asked.

"Well, a bunch of crazy people jump in frigid water to raise money for the library. It's mostly guys."

"Can't imagine why." I laughed. "When is it?"

"Saturday. I've got a good team together."

"I can't wait to see it."

A cocky smile spread across his lips.

"So tomorrow's the cookie exchange, and I still owe you for our last bet, so I'll be sure to deliver lots of baked goods before you freeze to death in the water."

"That's right. You wound up getting that Christmas tree I pointed out in the very beginning, but you were afraid of missing out on a better one. Seems to be a theme."

I shot him a playful glare.

"Anyway, I'll be sure to make good on my end of the bargain, but you still haven't come through on yours."

"What? The pickle and peanut butter sandwich?"

I nodded.

"You name the time and place, and I'll be more than happy to polish one off."

"Good."

His eyes fell to my lips, and the familiar charge pulsed through me.

"I've been thinking about you a lot," I told him.

"Is that so?" he asked, propping his leg on a stool.

"Yeah. I like our friendship."

"I definitely gathered that." He grinned.

"But I love the feelings that come over me when I think about you."

"What kind of feelings are those?"

"Well, it generally starts with an overall tingle, followed by a warmth that floods my entire body. It depends how long I let the fantasy go before—"

"Now it's a fantasy? Not just feelings?" He cut me off, his eyes darkening.

"Of course. Why wouldn't my thoughts be fantasies?"

He studied me carefully, and I slowly parted my lips, sliding my tongue along my bottom lip.

"Isn't a fantasy what transpires when you can't have the real thing?" I asked, moving closer to him.

His mouth curled into a dangerous grin.

"I think that's what a fantasy is, anyway." I shrugged my shoulders, standing less than a foot away.

Nick's eyes fell along my body before bringing them back to meet mine.

"What kind of fantasies do you have?" he asked, sliding his foot off the stool.

"Depends. Sometimes, I imagine us against the

wall. Other times, I think about the hot tub and how hard it was to behave myself that night."

"Well, you're not making it easy on me right now," he said in a low voice.

"I wasn't trying to make it difficult." I smiled. "I've done a lot of thinking since you were at my house last, and I've never experienced these feelings."

"What feelings in particular?"

"Uncontrollable lust."

He laughed.

"Is all this talk working?" I asked.

"You tell me," he growled, pulling me against him.

It certainly was doing the trick.

"Do you feel this way with your other friends?" I teased.

"Not in the slightest."

"Me neither." I giggled. "I'm tired of being scared of losing your friendship."

"You won't lose it."

"A thought did occur to me last night."

"What's that?" he asked.

"What if you're lousy in bed and I never call you back? Has that ever crossed your mind?" I placed both hands on my hips.

A smile crossed his lips. "Doubtful."

"It must be nice to be so confident in all things." Electricity ran through me, and I dropped my gaze.

He touched my chin and lifted it up.

"Some things are just fact." The familiar spark in his eye drilled a deeper longing into me.

"There's going to come a point when you're going to have make good on all these promises."

His hands ran under my jacket, and I knew I was close to getting what I wanted, but I needed to hear something. What made him visit his dad? I shifted my hand to his and took a deep breath.

"I have to confess that I thought last night I was going to come home and you were going to explain to me why you've done such a good job of putting me in the friend category."

"I've been putting you there because you wanted me to." His head cocked slightly.

"I don't think that's entirely true." I let out the breath I'd been holding. "I've never made out with my friends before."

Nick sat on a workbench and pulled me forward.

"You said yourself that you didn't want to lose our friendship."

"You forced that out of me last night. I was working through it just fine on my own." I chuckled. "Maybe slowly, but I was ready to jump into friends with benefits. Then you blew it." I giggled.

"Is that so?"

"For the record, I'm not a crier and I don't like that you saw that," I informed him. "I don't cry."

"There's nothing wrong with letting emotion show."

"I'm glad you said that." I wrapped my arms around his waist. "Because I think you're not telling me everything."

"About what?"

"Where did you go?" I asked softly.

"I feel like you already know." He studied me.

"So where did you disappear off to?" I asked him again.

"I wanted to check on my dad. I hadn't seen him in a while. He lives in Idaho."

"Oh?" I asked, draping my hands over his knees. "How'd it go?"

"About as well as I expected."

"Well, not all relationships are as glorious as mine and bird lady's."

He laughed, shaking his head.

"What? It's true."

"I'll have to remember that."

"I've been doing a lot of thinking, and having a holiday fling with my sexy neighbor would be a pretty spectacular Christmas present."

"A holiday fling," he repeated.

I nodded.

A flicker of desire dashed through his gaze as I tossed my jacket onto the dusty workbench, but he still didn't budge.

"I realized I've been lying to myself. Sure, I like my life, but everything is pretty surface-level. You know how your friendships back in the city were superficial? Well, I've developed the same pattern, but with relationships."

"You don't say."

"What I thought was fun was nothing more than a distraction."

"A distraction from what?" I asked.

He pressed his lips together. "What I really want out of life."

"Which is what?" I asked.

"I don't want to suffer through another holiday acting as if I'm completely happy and not missing out on something when I'm missing out on the one thing right in front of me." His eyes steadied on mine. "So I'll do anything you need just so I have you in my life."

I sank into the sweetness of his words, but I knew there was more.

"When my parents divorced, it jaded me on the idea of love and monogamy. If you don't promise it . . ."

My blood rushed through my veins.

"Have you cheated in the past?" I asked.

"Never, but my father did. A lot."

"That doesn't mean you will. You know the pain it caused your mom. You wouldn't do that."

"I hadn't seen my dad in years. I thought maybe it was time. I don't know what I expected, but I can tell you that what I saw was what I never want to become."

I nodded, waiting for more.

"What became apparent from the visit is that I've been a master at fooling myself into believing I'm truly happy." He looped his arms around my waist.

"There's nothing superficial about how your friends feel about you. They love you to pieces. I think you're quite happy."

"No, you're totally right about my friends. I'm lucky." His gaze fell to the floor. "But I've been wrong about what I want out of relationships." The darkness in his gaze returned as his eyes connected with mine.

"What is it you want, Nick?"

"I want you."

"Then you're in luck." I grinned, but he shook his head.

"I refuse to rush things."

"It would make sense that a man as oblivious about the central themes of a good eighties movie wouldn't have a clue about women."

He laughed.

"We're overthinking things," I told him.

"It's the safe thing to do, especially with something this important. We live across the street from each other. It's not easy to move."

I chuckled.

"What's the right thing to do?" I asked.

"I don't think there's a right and wrong here."

"Does that make us doubly screwed?" I slid my hand under his shirt, feeling the dips of his muscles beneath my fingertips.

"Possibly," he murmured.

"I was foolish to think I could ignore my sexy neighbor," I told him.

"Completely foolish," he agreed, moving his fingers along my hips and pulling me closer. He slid his fingers under my shirt, and a pulse of desire pulled me deeper into him.

"I've got some serious issues. How could I have resisted you for so long?" I teased.

He looked at me quizzically.

"Kiss me," I whispered. "Let's just have fun. Put everything aside and enjoy a good old-fashioned holiday fling."

"Are you sure about this, Holly?" he whispered in my ear.

"More than you can imagine."

Nick's eyes connected with mine as I ran my fingers through his hair. He slowly moved forward, but he didn't kiss me. He gently dragged his lips along my neck, and a shiver ran through me. His hands dipped lower, and my body trembled as his fingers skated between my skin and panties, teasing me, grazing me.

I pushed my fingers through his hair, bringing his mouth back to mine. The moment he kissed me, every worry about our future fell away.

His fingers explored me, leaving me completely breathless as his kisses deepened.

He slid off the workbench but lifted me on top, our kisses not even slowing as he slowly circled his fingers in all the right places. The sensations running over me made my entire body crave more, but his fingers slowed as he teased me, pushing and pulling me to the edge several times.

"I'm about—" I whispered, but his mouth pressed harder against mine as my body shuddered into his, my breathing ragged and my world spinning as he kept working to pull me over. I'd never experienced such insane pleasure before, and we were both fully clothed.

His kisses slowed, and I tried catching my breath as I blinked my eyes open to see him watching me.

"What's wrong?" I whispered.

"I can't do this." He shook his head. "I was

wrong." I felt his breathing steady, his arms still holding me tightly against him.

"About what?"

"I can't do casual with you. There's nothing casual about us, and I just made it like—" He stopped himself, and I was grateful for it.

I knew what he was going to say. He treated me like the others.

The worst part was that I felt comfortable in his arms, like this was where I belonged, and now he was shoving me away. I swallowed the last part down and closed my eyes, still resting my head on his chest.

"It's okay not to want a serious relationship. We've done well keeping things light. Just because it's the holidays, you don't have to rethink life. Count yourself lucky that you know what you want out of a relationship." I straightened up, looking at him.

"It's not about that," he said softly, shaking his head. "It has never been about that with you."

I saw the same pain in his gaze that I felt running through every fiber of my body, and I knew it didn't matter what I said. He'd already made up his mind.

Chapter Eighteen

I grabbed my purse and made my way out to the car, slyly looking to see if his truck was in the driveway.

It wasn't.

Maybe he reactivated his Tinder account.

Not that it mattered.

I slid into my car and took off toward Sophie's.

A girl's night couldn't have come at a better time.

By the time I'd arrived at Sophie's, I'd gotten myself all roiled up.

I tore up the steps and handed Sophie the tray of cookies as she opened the front door.

"I'm so ready for some holiday cheer." I grinned and took a deep breath, hearing Bing Crosby in the background.

"Well, we've got plenty." She smiled and

welcomed me inside.

Her home was gorgeous. Everything in her home was stunning yet perfectly homey. I saw a wall of windows overlooking Puget Sound, but it was too dark to actually see the water, just flecks of light in the distance.

"Your sister's not here yet. She said she's going to be a little late because she burned the first batch."

I chuckled. "Sounds about right. That's why I always volunteer to do baked goods."

I followed Sophie into the kitchen, and Natty jumped up from the table where she was constructing a gingerbread house.

"So good to see you. What can we get you to drink?" Her eyes were huge and she glanced over at Sophie.

They knew.

"I get that you're best friends, but seriously?" I groaned.

"I have no idea what you're talking about," Natty muttered.

Sophie poured me a cranberry and vodka and handed it to me.

"Good guess on the beverage." I took a sip.

"What can I say?" She ushered me to the table and pulled out a chair. Natty sat in front of the half-completed gingerbread house and let out a sigh.

"But I swear. Nick didn't say a word," Natty told me. "To either of us."

"It was more what he didn't say." Sophie drew in a breath. "I'm taking it his visit with his father didn't go well."

I shrugged. "I don't think it gave him the answers he was hoping for."

"So he called it off?" Sophie shook her head, not even waiting for my response. "Bastard."

Maybe that's all they were talking about.

"Well, I don't know. I mean, we didn't really have anything going. Just a kiss here or there, some harmless flirting." As I spoke, the knot in my stomach tightened. "He doesn't think he'll be able to be faithful. I'm assuming that was a thing with his dad?" I didn't want to admit what really happened. We went too far without both being on the same page. I pushed him there, and he fell into his same pattern and blames himself.

"Nick has never *not* been faithful." Natty groaned, shaking her head. "He's too considerate for his own good. Now, he's worrying about something that might never happen."

"His dad was a dog, but I don't know why Nick's all of a sudden worried about it." Natty put icing on a gumdrop and stuck it on the roof.

"Maybe he's been worried about it all along and that's why he gravitated toward Tinder," I offered.

"Could be, but I think he was more talk than not on Tinder hookups." Sophie poured a cup of punch. "This one time, he told me had a hot date in Seattle. Anthony and I happened to be headed to a gallery opening in the city. I shouldn't even be saying this."

"Now you have to." Natty laughed.

"Well, he was at the same opening all by

himself. He made up some excuse about his date canceling, but Anthony and I knew he was lying."

"Why in the world would he care?" Natty asked. "Why would he imply that he's dating when he's just wandering around an art show?"

I was wondering the same thing.

"The man's got a reputation to uphold," Sophie said with an exaggerated smile.

Natty shrugged.

"Hello." A new voice hummed through the air. I glanced toward the front of the house, and a redhead came bounding in with a platter of cookies.

"Our favorite teacher." Sophie hugged her and took the plate of cookies.

"Tori, this is Holly."

Tori's eyes grew huge, and I knew for a fact that she knew.

What, in particular, I wasn't sure.

"So good to meet you," I said, giving her a hug. "I feel like I already know you."

She laughed. "I could say the same."

My stomach clenched.

"We were just discussing Fireweed's favorite boy toy." Natty rolled her eyes.

"I don't know what's gotten into him." She grabbed a sugar cookie and took a bite.

"So is he acting differently?" I asked.

"Definitely. He's all over the place. Scattered." Tori studied me, and I realized she was indeed a schoolteacher. "You really like him."

"I feel very lucky to live across the street from him." I nodded.

"Yeah, Fireweed is known for nice neighbors, but that's not exactly what I was talking about."

Sophie handed me a refreshed drink and I took a gulp.

"I feel like I need backup. When did my sister say she was coming?" I joked and Natty chuckled. "I like him a lot. He's genuine, kind, caring, compassionate, and I pretty much spend all day thinking about him like I'm back in junior high."

"That's how it always begins," Sophie muttered.

Tori twisted her hair into a quick twist and took a seat.

"Well, I know I've never seen him this heartbroken." Tori took out her phone. "He texted me that he was grabbing a pizza for dinner and wondered if Mason, my fiancé, wanted any. He texted a sad face. Nick doesn't do sad faces."

So he and his truck were getting pizza tonight.

I let out a huff. "Well, he's the only one who can change that."

"I couldn't agree more." Tori nodded. "Mason always says you're either a pelican or a pelican't."

My gaze flashed to Sophie and she stifled a laugh. "There's a reason they're together. None of the rest of us find it amusing."

"Maybe the holidays are getting him down. Did you know he helped revive my parents' love connection? He planned a whole boat trip and paid for it and everything for them. I left a check on his porch, and he left it torn up on mine."

Sophie and Natty traded looks.

"What?" I questioned.

"You know, his parents split around Thanksgiving," Natty informed me.

"I doubt that would bother him after all these years," Tori argued. "He's never been down before during the holidays. Why now?"

Natty eyed me. "He's never had a Holly before."

"Well, all I can say is that I'd rather at least have a friendship with him than nothing else." I looked out the window and my reflection bounced back. "That's what I've been telling him all along. I don't want to screw up something so amazing."

Sophie rolled her eyes and shook her head. "Who knew two screwed-up people could find each other so easily?"

"I'm not screwed up." I frowned.

"Not screwed up, but possibly full of mixed signals," Natty offered.

"If Nick's trying to sort out which category Holly falls into, his head's going to explode," Tori added.

"I'm not that bad." I pouted. "He's the one who only sleeps with women in Seattle."

"Apparently, not any longer," Tori teased while Sophie and Natty's eyes widened.

"I—" I stopped, realizing she had no idea. She was just throwing it out there. "Not even."

"I know," Tori teased. "Or you'd be even more screwed up than I imagined."

Not even slightly funny.

The doorbell rang, and Sophie dashed through the kitchen. "That's either Jewels or your sister."

I didn't think I could handle four against one so I really hoped it was my sister.

My sister's voice rang through the home. "I tried to make Russian tea cookies, but all the powdered sugar melted."

"They'll be delicious," I assured her as she set the tray on the counter.

"We were just discussing the Nick and Holly debacle," Sophie said with a rueful look. "I really thought we had a match."

"I did too," my sister confessed.

"What?" I asked, my hands whipping to my hips.

"You heard me." My sister winked.

"Continue."

"I thought it was a match made in heaven. You seemed perfect for each other, and I swear, the chemistry. Wow. If only I could find that." My sister dropped her shoulders in disbelief.

"Can I just say that I feel really weird making this cookie exchange all about me?" I stood up and mixed another drink. The Fireweed Taxi service was going to be getting a call tonight.

"You didn't. We did," Sophie said just as the oven dinged. "I thought we might like some spinach dip too."

"Spinach dip and cookies. The absolute best Friday ever." Natty's phone buzzed, and she picked it up from the table.

"Someone's ears must have been ringing." She glanced up from her phone. "He convinced all the guys to go to the Mudflat Tavern."

I'd never been, but I knew right where it was and had a sudden itch to check it out.

"I smell the best mix of booze and sugar," Jewels said. I recognized her voice from my sister's house. "And a hint of . . . spinach?"

She bounced into the kitchen with not one but three trays of cookies.

"I just dropped Jake off at Mudflats. What the heck has gotten into Nick? He looked like a train ran him over."

My heart sank.

How in the world did we turn something fun and harmless into something overly serious? This had to change. I was fun. He was fun. I was cute. He was cuter. I didn't care what he was moping about. He was the only one who could fix it.

I marched over to Jewels' cookie trays and glared at them.

"What did they ever do to you?" she teased.

I chuckled. "Nothing. I was just thinking how best to snap Nick out of his funk."

"I bet all it would take is that lacy red bra," my sister threw out there.

"That made quite an impression," Jewels agreed.

"You heard about that?" I asked indignantly.

"From your sister." She laughed.

"But I heard about it from Nick." Sophie's smile grew far too large for her face.

"And so did I. Quite the impression. It made him watch *Flashdance*." Natty stood up.

My gaze shot to hers. "No, it didn't."

"Yeah. He watched it twice."

I groaned. "Are we as hopeless as we sound?"

"I'd say you're on the border." Amusement crossed my sister's features before she took one of Jewels' pizzelle cookies and snacked on it. "It melts in my mouth."

"Do you think we're going to have any cookies left to exchange?" I grabbed a pizzelle and had the same reaction as my sister.

"A few." Sophie hummed as she took the spinach dip out of the oven.

I wanted to round up as many cookies as I could to take them to Nick in the morning.

Who was I kidding? I wanted to deliver them tonight to his house. Why wait? Maybe I'd take them to Mudflats.

The rest of the night at Sophie's was a fun mix of celebrity gossip, since Natty and Sophie had the inside scoop, and island chatter. Time flew by, and I barely thought about Nick until I called the cab. As I put my platter of cookies together, Nick really crept under my skin. I wasn't going to go straight home. Nope, I was going to pop by the tavern and deliver cookies. After I said goodbye to everyone, I climbed in the cab and my nerves got the best of me. Maybe a surprise visit wasn't the best idea.

When the cab pulled up slowly to Mudflats, I saw the door swing open and my heart jumped a bit. Suddenly, I wasn't so sure what I'd find behind that door, and that worried me. He could be back to his old ways. I shook my head as I handed a twenty to the driver and asked him to wait.

I took in a deep breath and grabbed the platter of cookies I'd put together for him.

I might be a little foggy from all the festive drinks, but I knew I wasn't one to become easily swayed, confused or bamboozled.

I wasn't about to start now, not with Nick.

He liked me.

I liked him.

Besides being one the hottest men I'd ever met, he was one of the nicest, and I wasn't going to give up quite so easily. The more I thought about what we experienced, the more I became certain that we needed to let whatever was between us run its course. The worst thing to happen might be that I'd have to plant some extra-tall trees at the edge of my property.

End of story.

I hopped out of the car and paraded to the front door of the tavern. The Christmas lights made the place seem a little less intimidating, but the music rolling out the door every time someone opened it didn't.

As someone pushed open the door, I jumped out of the way, balancing my cookies, and convincing myself this was a good idea.

What I didn't expect was to see Andrea right in front of me.

I'd only seen her once, but it was enough of an interaction to get engrained.

Why in the world was she here? Thanksgiving had long since come and gone.

"Hey," she slurred. "You're the tea girl."

I stared at her, and she wobbled a little when her eyes landed on the cab.

"Cab's here," she hollered, and everything in me froze.

Who was she hollering to?

"Actually, that's my cab," I informed her.

And that's when I heard his voice, and it felt like my world crumbled.

Just a little bit.

Chapter Nineteen

"Can you help her to the cab and make sure she gets on the ferry back to Seattle?" I heard Nick's voice, but I didn't know where he was or who he was talking to until Anthony walked outside. I held the door open with my toe.

"Come on," Anthony said, guiding Andrea to my cab.

At this point, she could have it. Anything to get her away from Nick. I waved at the driver and he nodded. I think there were only two cabs on the entire island, so who knew how long it would take for the one she ordered to show up.

"Hey, Holly." Anthony grimaced as Andrea tripped over herself and into the cab. "Nick's inside."

"Thanks." I cleared my throat, trying to act

nonchalant as I slid through the door into the bar.

I saw a blinking Christmas tree in the corner and scanned the area. My eyes fell to Nick sitting with a group of guys across the room. My heart rate picked up as I made my way over and thought about what I was going to say.

Nothing very clever came to mind by the time I made it to the table. Three sets of eyes turned to me, but one stayed staring at the table.

"Surprise," I said, holding up the tray of cookies.

Nick immediately lifted his head, and the three other men shot up from the booth.

"You guys don't have to leave," I said, shaking my head.

"Tori texted that she's on her way home," one of them told me.

"So you must be Mason." I smiled.

"In the flesh." He grinned, and I could perfectly imagine him sliding the one-liner about pelicans to Tori.

"I'm Jake and that's Cole." Jake pointed at the guy next to him. They were all attractive guys, but nothing like Nick.

Nick was just perfection.

Even the way the Christmas lights twinkled off his face made me enamored. He was purely hard to ignore.

"All the girls did an amazing job," I told them. "You're going to love the cookies."

I felt Nick's gaze on me, but he still hadn't said anything.

I turned to look at Nick, and happiness squished into me merely from being around him.

"I don't doubt it." Jake's lip quirked up slightly as he led me into the booth, taking the tray of cookies and setting them on the table.

Anthony punched Nick in the shoulder. "Good luck, man."

Good Luck?

I glanced at his beverage.

"Water?" I asked, smiling.

"Surprised?"

"Well, you're at a bar." I wiggled my brows.

"And you were at a cookie party." He grinned, looking at the cookies. "And who's the one with the googly eyes?"

"My eyes aren't googly." I sat back in the booth and squirmed against the leather seat.

"How'd you get here?" he asked.

"A cab." My stomach sloshed. "The same cab Andrea left in."

Nick let out a groan.

"Has she decided to move here?" I teased.

"I hope not." He shook his head.

"Me too."

"Most women would be tearing my head off right about now." Nick laughed.

"I thought we established that I'm not most."

"That's an understatement." He nodded.

"But I am curious what brings her here."

"That Polar Bear Dip I mentioned?" he asked, and I nodded. "Well, when she was last here, she signed up her company to sponsor it."

"Another way to pay a visit?"

"I suppose."

I didn't like that she was at the bar with Nick and I wasn't, but I was relieved that it didn't appear he fell into his old ways.

"So what brings you to Mudflats?"

"Well, prior to running into your girlfriend, I was ready to let you have it." I was tempted to order a hard cider.

"And after?" he asked.

"I'm still ready to let you have it, but for a different reason."

"Well, there you go. Let me have it." He cocked his head and waited.

"I can't."

"Why's that?" He snuck his finger under the plastic wrap and snagged the raspberry thumbprint cookie I'd made. "My favorite."

"Of course they are, and that's precisely why I *can't* let you have it. We are perfect for each other."

"You've totally lost me."

"As I was eating cookies and talking endlessly about you with your best friends, I realized we were both doing the same thing, just in different ways." I snuck a cookie too. "We're both trying to find a reason to delay the inevitable."

"What's the inevitable?"

"You tell me."

"If only I knew." He laughed. "Before you moved in across the street, I had life figured out." He bit his lip, and I cocked my head, studying him. His eyes held a darkness that made my body tense. "I love what I do for a living and I have a great group of friends. Life is good. It's entertaining, interesting, never dull." He ran his fingers along his cheek, highlighting a day or two of missed shaves.

"So you liked your life better before I moved to town?" I gave a nervous laugh. "This conversation is off to a great start."

His eyes flashed to mine.

"My life was a perfectly played habit, a continual loop always landing me in the same predicament with the same problem. I knew that with you, I was going to go about things differently." He shook his head and a wry smile crossed his expression. "And then I screwed it up."

I didn't like thinking that what we'd experienced at his workshop was a habit, but I also knew we both didn't live in a monastery.

"So I'm not the first?" I pretended to act shocked.

He ran his teeth over his bottom lip, and desire washed over me so I looked away.

"I think I get where you're coming from, but you let Andrea walk out." I slid a sideways glance in his direction. "That could have been an easy—"

"I had her escorted out," he corrected.

I had to admit I loved hearing that. Asking him to repeat it probably wouldn't be very mature.

"This is the deal. I like you. You like me. I'm over my stuff and am willing to take a chance. You, however, are getting more complicated by the second." I shifted on the bench. "What changed so instantly after . . ." I didn't want to finish.

"Seeing how perfect you were in that moment." He drew a breath. "I knew I was falling in love with you."

The words rocked the world around me as I stared at Nick.

"Why would that make you pull back?" I questioned.

"You're not even close to being to that point, and I've never been there before." He groaned. "I thought being around you was better than not, but I realized I was wrong."

"You've never been in love before?" I asked.

"Never."

"By design," I told him, realizing why Tinder played such an intense part of his social life. "You wouldn't allow yourself to fall for anyone."

"Until you."

I shook my head. "Except you're still not letting yourself fall or you wouldn't have pushed me away."

"I don't want the love to run out." He sucked in his lip and glanced over at the Christmas tree.

"So it's easier not to love in the first place. Is that why you helped with my parents?" I asked.

"Any couple whose biggest problem is a bird coming between them still has a shot. There's still love there. It just needed to be brought to the surface again." He grinned.

"How do you know these things? Aren't you a man above it all?" I asked.

"I saw it with my parents. They ran out of

love." He sucked in a deep breath, but he didn't let it out.

"My parents had such a passionate relationship when I was a kid. They had so much fun together." He smiled. "But by the time I reached high school, it was like it had all drained from them. They were two miserable souls by the end of it. I still don't understand what led either of them to behave as they did."

"That's what makes you so skeptical about love?" I asked. "You don't think it will last?"

"I suppose." He shrugged. "I never gave it much thought until you. That's why I visited my dad. That's why I got so pissed off that I couldn't control myself around you."

"I don't want you to control yourself around me."

He let out a low growl.

"Don't you ever wish we could turn back time?" I asked.

"Like to the eighties?" Nick teased.

I liked the spark surfacing in his gaze again. This was the Nick I'd come to know and love.

"Maybe." A smile slid on my lips.

"What do you love so much about that decade?" he asked, stretching in the booth.

I pressed my lips together and thought hard about it.

"I was in grade school." I smiled.

"That's it? You just love the eighties because you were in elementary school?"

"No." I bunched my face to hide whatever emotion might flicker across it. "I liked it then because I didn't bother to recognize things that annoyed me. I just bounced from one happy event to the next. I didn't have time to overanalyze and second-guess life because I was too busy watching *Fraggle Rock* or playing with Barbies. Basically, I was too busy enjoying life. I liked that version of myself the best. The music, the movies, my friends, family—it was all a focus in that era. It's not like the third-grade me was like, oh wow, how can I learn to create stock portfolios for people so they can have a solid retirement? Yet, that's what my life turned into. Probably doesn't make any sense."

"It makes perfect sense."

I shrugged. "So that's the version of myself I hope to get back to someday."

"That's the version I see in you already."

"How so?" I asked.

"You're such a free spirit, Holly. I've never met a woman who is so quick to take a bet, to strip into a hot tub, to sing and dance in her—"

I held up my hand. "Point taken."

A hint of laughter sparked in his eyes.

"So why don't we blow this pop stand?" I asked.

"And do what?"

"Anything that doesn't involve thinking. I'm pretty sure it's more trouble than it's worth."

He stood up, grabbed the tray of cookies, and helped me out of the booth. The liquor was still swimming through my veins, and I took a second to get my bearings.

"You ready for me to take you home?" he

asked.

"Only if you don't leave once we get there." I curled my fingers into his bicep as he led me out of Mudflats, and with every step forward, excitement pulsed through me.

"And no more long talks until tomorrow." I chuckled, buckling my seatbelt as he climbed in. "It only makes things stall."

"You don't want things to stall?" He laughed.

"Not after the treat in Santa's workshop." I giggled.

"How much have you had to drink?"

"Too much."

He placed his hand on my knee, and this time, there was something less innocent with his touch as his fingers slid up my thigh and rested there until we got home.

The drive home was fewer than ten minutes, but by the time we got inside, I could barely think straight. I opened the door and nearly tumbled out of the truck in my excitement.

"I'm not going anywhere. Promise." He chuckled, helping me up the steps.

"You'd better not, or you really would have to move, and you have a lovely house."

I slid my key into the door and pushed it open, feeling his hands already sliding along my waist and creating the stir of emotions I'd grown so used to pushing away, but this time, I let them coast over me.

"We have a slight problem again," I murmured.

"What's that?"

"No bed."

His mouth curled into a smile. "Beds are overrated."

"Good." I turned around, my back facing him, as I pulled off my sweater, wearing the same red bra as the first night we met.

I heard his breath catch, and my pulse quickened. He closed the door and came up behind me.

"Holly," he whispered. "I've wanted you from the moment I first saw you."

"Then what took you so long?" I murmured.

He let out a slow and sexy grumble as he swept my hair to the side.

I giggled and felt heat roll up my body as his warm breath scattered across my neck, his lips slowly caressing my skin.

Between his words and the soft kisses he dotted along my neck, my world filled with a need I'd never experienced before. He turned me around, and I slowly ran my hand down his abdomen, down to the bulge beneath his jeans.

I slowly unbuttoned his jeans, and he brought his mouth back to mine, kissing me harder as my body ground into his.

"I need you," I breathed between kisses. "The chair."

I dropped the blanket on the chair and gently pushed him down, hovering over him. I needed to be in control.

Surprise flashed across his gaze, but the fire behind his eyes intensified as he pulled me onto him. I straddled his lap and rested my arms behind him.

His eyes locked on mine before he coiled his fingers through my hair, bringing me closer, tasting me and making my entire world spin into a reckless craze of emotion.

My fingers quickly unzipped his pants, and he shook them off as I pulled his shirt over his head. Nick tore his lips away from mine and then brought me into his arms, but I shook my head.

I climbed off the chair and took a step back, trying to memorize everything about him, and it was like he was doing the same. His eyes skated down my entire body. He followed my hands as I unbuttoned my pants, and I continued to keep my gaze on him.

His broad shoulders led my eyes down to his pecs, and my stomach twisted with excitement as my gaze went lower. He was . . .

Beautiful.

I kicked off my pants and bent down, kissing him, feeling my body ache for more before I even bothered to wait for an invitation.

"Holly," he breathed. "Slow down."

But I couldn't. Everything I'd been dreaming about was in front of me.

He pulled me up, and his mouth moved along my throat to my chest. He unhooked my bra and freed my breasts, breathing in deeply as he took me in.

Nick slowly worked his tongue along my nipples, and my body shuddered from desire. What he did with his tongue was hypnotizing. His hands slid along my belly and moved toward my hips, his fingers crushing into me as I circled my body over his.

"God, Holly." He drew in a sharp breath as I dipped my legs lower without letting him enter. "You feel so amazing."

His words did more to me than anything. His fingers hooked my panties and rolled them to the side.

I leaned back and his gaze traveled up my body. Warmth rushed over my flesh as his hands shook from the desire stirring between us.

I moved over him, my mouth fitting to his as I eased deeper onto his lap. His fingers slid along my bare skin, causing my body to ripple with expectation.

I stretched back, and his teeth raked across my belly, sending a wave of shivers across my body. Nick's arms stayed looped around my waist as I arched backward. His groans intensified as my body rocked with his. My thighs locked around his legs as I brought myself back up, quickening my pace when his breathing hitched, but instead of releasing, he curled his fingers through my hair, bringing my lips to his. Every desire I'd been denying myself came crashing out as my body moved in the same rhythm as his.

As I buried myself into this world, I felt his hips thrust into me, and I lost complete control, the control I'd tried so hard to keep as my own.

"Nick," I said, breathless and dizzy as the first of many sensations flooded through my body as his hips kept grinding into mine.

I blinked my eyes open to see him throw his head back, his jaw clenching in ecstasy. I never felt so full as my body collapsed onto his. Nick's breathing was fast, his body slick, and I didn't want to be anywhere else.

Chapter Twenty

"So how's everything going?" Maddie asked.

"Good." I nodded, pulling my wool gloves back on.

It was freezing outside, but apparently, the Polar Bear Dip wasn't to be missed by anyone on the island. Most of the town closed shop early so we could watch people jump into the icy water.

Even though it was late afternoon, Christmas lights sparkled from several food and beverage stands, and a huge fire had been started in the park we were in so the sane could keep warm.

Stacks of red and green towels were placed on long tables, along with bottled waters and protein bars. I wasn't sure if I was at a marathon or a dip in the cold water.

Several businesses had booths in the park too.

There was a bank handing out t-shirts, an energy drink company giving away drinks, two restaurants handing out samples, a technology company handing out fridge magnets, and of course, the library selling used books. I knew this because I'd stalked them all and grabbed my free stuff. I wasn't sure which company Andrea worked for, but I was careful to keep a watchful eye for her.

The group of spectators was growing, and I kept looking for any sign of Nick.

"This seems crazy." Maddie chuckled.

"It really does, but it's for a good cause," I told her.

"What's got you so chipper?" she asked.

"I've got a little surprise." I smiled.

"What are you talking about?" Her blues eyes twinkled with intrigue.

"Tori said the donations were down, so we're going to see about changing that."

I tugged on the neckline of my sweater and snapped my bikini strap underneath.

"You're kidding. You're going to jump in?"

"We'll see. I'm kind of letting Jewels plan it. I just told her I'd show up in my bikini. I've decided I need to make a better effort when it comes to making friendships."

My sister laughed. "Definitely one way to go about it. I bet you'll be making all kinds of friends today." She wiggled her brows just as a man using a bullhorn started shouting that the event was about to start.

I stood on my toes and tried to see over

everyone's heads to find Nick and still came up empty-handed.

"There's Tori and Sophie," I told my sister and waved, trying to get their attention.

Sophie grinned and hopped up and down, waving for us to come over.

We wound our way through the crowd as the announcer asked the participants to move toward the water.

My pulse elevated slightly because I didn't actually know what was in store. Jewels said that before the dip, she was going to announce a twist, but I had no idea what my part was.

Out of the corner of my eye, I saw Andrea making her way through the crowd. She had a tag hanging around her neck, so I assumed that meant she was jumping. She was dressed in short shorts and a tight camisole.

Perfect outfit for winter.

Jewels had the roster of participants, so she knew Andrea had signed up. My heart squeezed a little more for my new friends. She wanted me to outshine Andrea, and something told me I just might.

"Where are the guys?" I asked Sophie.

"Making themselves pretty, I'm guessing." She looked over my shoulder and smiled. Just as I was about to turn around, someone pressed their palms over my eyes from behind.

"Hey, you," Nick said.

"Hey." I grinned, wondering why he was making it so I couldn't see.

"You have to promise me you won't think less

of me for what I'm about to show you," Nick instructed.

I heard the other men giving everyone else the same lines around me, with Sophie squealing in fear and Natty panicking.

"I don't know that I'd make that promise." Maddie laughed.

"Is it that bad?" I asked.

"It's not great," she teased. "I think the image is burned into my mind forever."

I giggled and let out an exaggerated sigh. "Okay, I promise. You're still the stud of Fireweed, Nick."

Nick dropped his hands and spun me around.

I opened my eyes and saw Nick standing in front of me in a red union suit, which would have been unique in itself, but it was what was underneath that made the most impact as he unzipped the pajamas even lower.

"How in the world did you find a Rudolph speedo?" I asked.

"A lot of dedication and determination."

I started laughing and couldn't stop.

I glanced at the horrified expressions on Tori, Natty, and Sophie's faces as their men stood in front of them, and I knew this had been in the works for a while.

"It's good you started to make your moves before this," I joked, still unable to control my laughter.

"Jumpers, please make your way to the dock."

"I guess that's my cue." He beamed.

"I think it is."

I saw Andrea watching us, and my insides burned. I think Andrea might be one of those women who didn't like the person until they realized someone else did.

Nick followed my gaze and groaned.

"She doesn't get the message very easily," he grumbled.

"Let's not have it ruin our fun." I stood on my toes and gave him a quick kiss on the cheek.

"Could we please have Holly Wildes come forward?" the man asked, and Nick shot me a puzzled look.

"You're not the only one full of surprises." I grinned.

"Holly Wildes is our special guest and one of our newest residents on Fireweed," Jewels took over speaking in the bullhorn. "And this year, we have a little surprise to make our fundraiser a little more exciting."

My pulse spiked as I thought about what she had in mind.

Nick stayed close behind as I worked my way through the crowd and over to Jewels. I spun around and looked at the audience. There were hundreds of people standing and staring, waiting for Jewels to continue.

My eyes found Nick's, and I couldn't help but smile wider.

"So we have a little auction going on. We know most of you here in the crowd are spectators waiting to witness complete insanity. Well, we're a little behind on this year's goal." Jewels scanned the crowd, and I brought my gaze back to Nick's. "I'm giving you participants or spectators a chance to jump into the ice-cold water holding Miss Holly Wildes."

Nick's eyes grew twice their size, and his arm shot into the air, followed by several other men I didn't recognize.

"Do I hear one hundred to jump into the water with Holly?" Jewels asked.

"Two hundred," Nick called out.

Some guy about ten feet away called out three hundred, and my self-confidence started to blossom.

"Do I hear three hundred and fifty?" Jewels asked into the bullhorn.

I glanced at my sister, who was laughing. I shrugged and tugged my sweater over my head, tossing it on the dock. I wasn't actually in that great of shape, but I'd ordered a green bikini that hid all the flaws in case I hopped in Nick's hot tub again. Little did I know I'd be showing it off in front of a few hundred of my neighbors.

"Four hundred," Nick called out.

I kicked off my jeans, readying myself for the cold water.

A spectator hollered five hundred, and I stared at Nick, hoping he'd come up.

"A thousand," Nick said, taking a few steps forward from the crowd.

"Do I have anything over a thousand?" Jewels asked.

The crowd started cheering, and my cheeks flushed from the attention as Nick walked up and scooped me into his arms.

"You never cease to amaze me," he whispered, and my heart filled with joy.

"That's how I hope to keep it."

The rest of the participants began stripping off their shirts and sweatpants in anticipation for what was about to come. Agreeing to this seemed like a much better idea over cookies and drinks. Now the fear was literally pummeling through me. I wasn't ready to die in ice cold water.

"You ready for this?" he asked me, and I shook my head, bracing for the icy waters as he carried me down the dock.

"This year, we raised over five thousand dollars thanks to these crazy participants who are willing to freeze a little," the announcer began as all the people began filing down the dock behind us.

A little.

A little. I'll only be freezing a little.

When we reached the end of the dock, Nick set me down and began stripping out of his onesie.

"It didn't get any better." I giggled.

"What can I say?" He grabbed my hand. "But like with the rest of life, let's not overthink it."

He didn't even give me a second to protest as he jumped in, pulling me in with him.

It was so cold, it felt like tiny shards of glass poking into my flesh, but before the real pain set in, Nick was already pulling me out of the water and drying me off with towels. I looked all around as people began dropping off the dock one by one.

A volunteer brought over hot apple cider and I began trying to drink it to warm up.

My teeth began chattering, and Nick pulled me into him as my sister brought my sweater and jeans.

"What was I thinking?" I asked in between chatters as we made our way to the fire.

"You wanted to impress me." He grinned.

"You think?"

"Pretty sure."

"Did it work?"

"It did."

I glanced around and didn't see Andrea anywhere.

Thank goodness. Maybe she finally got the picture.

"Do you have any plans for Christmas?" Nick asked as the warmth from the flames began to make the shivering stop.

I glanced at my sister, who was over talking to Jewels as she attempted to dry off Jake. Another guy walked up to them, and his eyes stayed on my sister.

"I don't. My parents are taking a river cruise, so it's just me and my sister for the holidays."

"Is that so?"

I nodded. "They've found a great bird sitter. I can't even begin to thank you for—"

"It was nothing."

"But it turned into something, so thank you. I think things could have gone in a really terrible direction."

He smiled wider.

"I thought maybe we could spend Christmas Eve together."

"What about Christmas Day?" I asked.

"I thought one would roll into the other."

"That's the kind of thinking ahead I like." I looped my arms around Nick's neck and smiled. "So do you know who that guy is over there talking to my sister?"

"That's Jake's brother, Chance." He smiled. "He lives on Hound Island."

"Interesting."

"Why's that?"

"Hildie has been trying to get us to visit her lavender farm for quite some time, and now I think I know why."

Chapter Twenty-One

"**A**re you sure there needs to be that many pickles on it?"

I smeared the last swirl of peanut butter on the empty slice of bread.

"Positive. That's what all the cookbooks say. Eight pickles." I sliced it in half and handed him the plate. "Go for it."

He took in a big breath and took the first bite, followed by a second.

"Not as bad as you thought?" I asked.

"It could be worse."

"Exactly." I nodded and put the peanut butter and pickles back in my fridge.

It was three days until Christmas, and I felt like I was in heaven. Turning from neighbors, to friends, to this—we left it nameless—was the best decision of our lives, and I spoke for both of us.

Nothing changed about our friendship, except that it grew in ways I couldn't even explain in only a matter of days. Nick was still the loyal, caring and kind man he was before we slept together, but now I'd say he was even more so.

I glanced at his empty plate.

"Nice work."

"I always make good on my bets."

"And so do I." I put his dish in the sink.

"I've been thinking," he started, and I froze.

"Don't do that." I shook my head. "We need to just go with the flow."

He laughed and pulled me into him.

"I've been thinking that I'd like you to come over to my house tonight. You've been cooking nonstop for me since the Polar—"

"That's because you spent a thousand dollars. I feel bad. I want to make it up to you."

"I *donated* a thousand dollars, and the library can always use it."

"Still, I thought you might toss in a fifty. I never expected to have so many bidders. Who knew I was such a catch?"

"I did." He laughed and nuzzled his nose against mine. "I did."

"Okay, so a date tonight?" I glanced at the clock.

I had twenty minutes until I needed to be at the store. Not enough time for the things running through my head.

"What time?" I asked.

"As soon as you get off." He gave me a tender

kiss, which only stirred up more emotion.

"You make it very difficult to earn a living," I whispered, giving him one more kiss.

I grabbed my bag and he followed me out of the house.

"I've got a huge order I need to get done today, so I might not have my phone where I can reach it," he told me.

"Okay," I said, giving him one more kiss before I hopped in the car.

Maddie had taken yesterday off. She didn't tell me why, but I had my suspicions after seeing Chance show up at the Polar Bear Dip.

I cranked up Madonna singing *Santa Baby* and pulled out of the driveway and onto the main road. The clouds above had turned from a frothy gray to a crisp white, and something told me a white Christmas was on the way.

I found a parking spot across the street from the tea shop and saw my sister already inside the store, turning on the twinkle lights and flipping the sign to *Open*.

The road was still pretty empty at this time, so I didn't bother with the crosswalk and got inside in record time.

"Good morning, happy sister," I called into the store.

She poked her head out and smiled. "Good morning."

"Did you see that giant order that came in for January?" I asked.

"I did. I'll place the order for the herbs this afternoon." She wasn't really making eye contact, which intrigued me.

"So how's Chance?" I asked.

"What?" She blushed.

"Jake's brother? How's he doing?"

"Fine."

"So I think I know why Hildie wants us to visit. *Us* really meaning you." I chuckled.

"Doubtful."

I shrugged. "We'll see."

"So I'm guessing you and Nick got over that friendship hurdle?" She was definitely changing the subject.

"We did, and it only made things better. He's making me dinner tonight at his house."

"I don't know how to bring this up, so I'll just say it."

The way her tone changed, I wasn't sure that I wanted to hear anything.

"Is it about Nick?"

"It's about Christmas."

"What about it? I was thinking we could do it at my house. Nick will probably—"

"Hildie invited me to the farm. I guess they have a huge celebration that begins on Christmas Eve and goes until the 26th."

I stared at her in surprise. "Yeah. Totally."

"I mean, I think it would be good for business relations. She's been after us to come over for so long."

"Oh, absolutely," I nodded, trying to keep the smile off my face. "Definitely should do it for the sake of the tea shop."

She narrowed her eyes at me. "I'm serious."

"I know you are, which makes it even cuter."

She rolled her eyes, but a smile crept over her lips. "Her son is pretty good-looking, and he seems so passionate about what he does for a living."

"And so do you."

She smiled. "Do you mind covering for me on the 26th?"

"Nope. It's my job to make your life easier." Just as I turned around, the first swarm of customers came in, and it never let it up until quitting time.

I was fully exhausted and looked like I'd just been through a tornado. My sister didn't look any better. Most of our teas ran out, which meant we'd be coming in early to make more. I always heard about the Christmas madness, but I guess until a person works retail, they just wouldn't understand.

The thought of seeing Nick tonight was both exhilarating and worrisome. I was exhausted and I didn't know what he had planned. Actually, that thought was kind of invigorating.

"Why do you have such a dopey look on your face?" my sister asked, tossing me my purse.

"I don't."

"Whatever you say," she joked.

I locked up the store and walked across the street. There were several restaurants along our road, and all of them were packed. I absolutely loved the week before Christmas. It was like the world went into slow motion and people stopped to enjoy one another's company.

By the time I pulled into my driveway, all my worry about being too tired was swept to the side and I couldn't wait to see Nick. I ran inside my house, showered, put on a cute pair of jeans and a red cashmere sweater, and quickly made my way over to his house.

I knocked on the door, but he didn't answer so I rang the bell.

Still nothing.

Maybe he was out back. I peered into one of the windows and saw only a faint glow coming from the back of the house. I tried the door and it was open.

The second I stepped inside, my heart literally skipped a beat.

I couldn't believe what I was hearing as I walked into the foyer and listened to Asia's *Heat of the Moment* roll through the air. I followed the music into the family room, where he was sitting on the couch, waiting for me with a pair of Ray Bans on.

I started giggling and shook my head.

"You know you're inside, right?"

He stood up and slowly walked over to me. My smile only grew when I saw him in a pair of stone-washed acid jeans with rips all over and a tattered bomber jacket.

"I wasn't sure if I should go for the Miami Vice look or . . ." his voice trailed off and I glanced at the screen, where *The Breakfast Club* was playing.

"You did all this for me?" I asked.

He bent down and grabbed something off the

coffee table.

"Appetizer?" he asked.

I looked down to see packages of strawberry Pop Rocks.

"No way."

"Yes, way." He slid back his sunglasses as I ripped open a packet and sprinkled the candies in the back of my mouth. The popping and sizzling made me way too excited for my own good, and I let out a soft moan.

"I'll have to remember these in the future." He smiled. "I have pizza rolls in the oven."

"Are you serious?"

"I had to make it authentic. I grew up on Smurfberry Crunch, but I couldn't find it."

"I loved that stuff. There's so much eighties awesomeness that went away with the decade, but I can't believe you went to this much effort."

"You haven't seen anything yet." He laughed as the music looped, and I threw my head back in laughter. "Right this way."

He led me up the stairs and into his bedroom, where there were several wrapped packages.

"I can't be the one to have all the fun." He motioned toward his clothes and slid the first box toward me.

"Are you serious?" I asked, sliding my finger under the giftwrap.

I lifted the lid off and couldn't keep in my glee at the hot pink pair of leg warmers and matching fingerless gloves.

"You like?" he asked, kneeling next to me and shoving another one over to me.

"Love." I opened the next one that had at least a hundred black jelly bracelets, an oversized gray sweatshirt, and a pair of leggings. "No way."

"I have a confession."

I moved my gaze slowly to his. "What's that?"

"I loved the eighties too. I have *Top Gun* and can recite most scenes. I didn't have to go out to buy *The Breakfast Club* or *Sixteen Candles.* I had them both. One of my favorite Christmas movies is *Gremlins*, right along with *National Lampoon*. I think the best action movies to exist were made in the eighties. You can't beat *Rambo* or *Die Hard*." He let out an exasperated sigh. "It's a dirty little secret of mine."

"It's not dirty." I shook my head, looping the jelly bracelets over my wrists. "It's perfection."

His eyes stayed on mine.

"But if you had told me this when we first met, I would've blown right past friendship to—"

"Then it's good I didn't tell you. I wouldn't want to change how we came to be for one second."

"Really?"

The swell of emotion was overwhelming. I was falling in love with this man.

The oven dinged.

"I'll meet you downstairs?" he asked, and I nodded.

To have found a guy who was this considerate was mind blowing. The closest I'd ever gotten to romance and thoughtfulness was a boyfriend remembering I actually had a birthday. For someone to go to this much trouble for no reason was absolutely amazing.

I glanced at my new jewelry and smiled. Yeah. Sometimes, things were meant to be.

How else could I explain moving into a cabin across the street from the sexiest and most notorious bachelor on the island? Yet, with all of his rules and all of my hang-ups, we managed to get here, a place where we belonged.

I stood up in a trance, stripped my sweater off, pulled the sweatshirt over my head, tugged off my pants, and pulled on my leggings. The final touches were the leg warmers and gloves. The fact that I didn't care what I looked like spoke volumes as I traipsed down the stairs to see him mixing a salad as the pizza rolls cooled off.

"You look sensational," he said, his eyes running along my leggings.

"Why, thank you." I walked into the kitchen and snagged a pizza roll off the tray.

"I can't wait to strip you out of them. I have an entire playlist ready and waiting."

"You really know how to make a girl feel special." I chuckled, walking over to him.

He turned around and slowly moved me away from the hot tray.

"Dinner can wait," he said. "Seeing you in these . . ."

I laughed, looping my arms around his neck. "I honestly think the eighties need to make a comeback."

"Well, tonight they will."

Chapter Twenty-Two

"Take good care of her," I told Jake.

"Will do." Jake smiled and pulled Jewels into him as my sister sat in the helicopter. She was terrified, but the ride was purely for the sake of the business.

"And if the snowstorm comes in like they expect—" I began.

"We'll all be staying on Hound Island." Jake winked.

I nodded and sucked in a nervous breath. It was Christmas Eve, and a snowstorm was set to arrive in the morning.

There was a lot left to learn about Jake Harlen, but finding out he had a chopper was certainly unexpected.

My sister blew me a kiss, and I waved as Nick roped his arms around my waist.

"The sooner you let them go, the better," Nick whispered, and I nodded.

"Well, Merry Christmas, and please tell your mom thank you for hosting my sister." I smiled.

"I think there are some ulterior motives there, but who am I to stand in the way?" Jake laughed, throwing up his hands.

Jewels gave me a quick hug. "We'll take good care of her."

I watched Jewels climb into the helicopter, and Jake shut the door before he walked around and climbed in on his side.

"Let's move back," Nick said, squeezing me tightly. "She'll be fine. Jake is an expert pilot. You should hear about some of his adventures."

I froze. "Not what I want to hear."

Nick chuckled, and we walked toward our car as I heard the helicopter roar to life. I glanced behind me. The swooping of the blades made my stomach clench.

"Promise me you won't take that up as a hobby," I muttered.

"You've got my word. That's some crazy shit." He grinned, and I crawled into his truck as the chopper lifted off the ground. They were pointed in the opposite direction, but I still waved until she was out of view.

"It's kind of weird not having my sister around for the holidays. Same with my parents."

He turned on the engine and glanced over at me. "I was worried that might happen."

My phone buzzed, and I saw a text slide over from my parents.

Wishing you a Merry Christmas! We miss you and

hope you're having a wonderful time with your boyfriend.

I showed Nick the text.

"I like how that looks." He pulled down the drive, and I immediately felt better. We may not all be in the same spot this year, but we were still family.

I glanced at Nick and my insides warmed. I had a lot to be grateful for this year.

I began texting back.

I miss you! Maddie is on her way to Hound Island. Nick and I are on our way back home for a cozy night. Love you and Merry Christmas!

My mom texted back.

Love you and I hope you like your present.

I glanced at Nick. I wondered what she was talking about. Come to think of it, nothing actually arrived from my parents, which was odd in itself.

Jake's house was on the far end of the island, so by the time we got back to the house, it was almost dark, but my cozy cabin was blazing in Christmas lights.

Nick parked in front of the house, and I couldn't imagine a better Christmas Eve. Life just felt right.

We had a pork loin in the oven, presents under the tree, and new beginnings to last a lifetime.

"Holly," Nick said, turning to face me.

"Yeah?" I asked.

"I just want you to know that you've made my dreams come true."

"Dreams?" I asked.

He nodded and glanced at my cabin.

"Fireweed is my favorite place in the world. I couldn't imagine living anywhere else, but there was always something missing."

"What was missing?"

"You." He moved closer, his lips moving to mine. I felt the intensity behind his kiss, and I knew we'd both finally found what we'd been looking for.

Each other.

When our fingers were cold and our lips numb, Nick's kisses slowed, and I took a deep breath, looking at him with a dopey expression.

"Now, you have to close your eyes," Nick instructed.

"What? In the car?" I asked.

"You can get out of the car, but then you have to close them."

I glanced around the yard.

"Are you sure about this? I might trip."

"I'll make sure you don't." He smiled and slid out of the truck, and I clamped my lids shut. He opened my door, and I felt him secure his hands around my waist and lift me to the ground.

A man of his word, he got me to the front door, unlocked it, and led me safely inside.

The smell of pork loin and apples filled my tiny space.

"Can I open my eyes?"

"Nope." He began leading me through the family room and down the hall to my bedroom. "Okay, keep them closed," Nick whispered, anchoring me in place.

He let go, and I heard his footsteps leave and scurry back.

"Okay, Holly Wildes. Merry Christmas."

I blinked my eyes open to see my bedroom completely transformed.

The sleigh bed he'd been working on in his workshop was by my window with a matching bedside table on each side, and a wardrobe in the corner. A white fluffy goose down comforter was draped over the bed, and layers and layers of red and white pillows were piled on top.

I was in shock. I couldn't even begin to imagine the time it took him to complete all these pieces.

"Do you like it?" he asked, and I realized I hadn't moved a muscle or said a word

"I'm completely awestruck," I whispered, pushing down the lump in my throat. "I can't even believe it. This is the most beautiful bedroom ever. This is the most special present ever."

"I love you, Holly. I wanted our first Christmas to be special."

"Just being with you is special, Nick. This is

spectacular." Nick drifted over my way and brought me into him. "I love you, Nick. Everything about you. How did you even do this? My room was empty just a couple of hours ago."

"Well, I think your friend list is growing. Sophie, Anthony, Cole, and Natty all rushed over to make it happen while we were gone."

"Are you serious? They moved furniture on Christmas Eve for you?" I stood in shock.

"No, Holly. They did it for you. Welcome to Fireweed." His eyes glinted with satisfaction.

"I'll never leave," I whispered, shaking my head.

"That's music to my ears."

I noticed an envelope on my bed.

"Is that from my parents?" I asked, recognizing the penmanship.

Nick sucked on his lip.

"Now this is where it gets interesting."

"How so?"

We walked over to the bed, and I snatched the envelope up and glanced at Nick. He had a worried expression on his face.

"Should I be as worried as you look?"

"It depends."

I slid my finger along the edge, pulled out the card, and opened it up.

There was a photo of a home overlooking the water.

"I don't get it." I glanced at Nick.

"Flip over the picture."

My eyes fell to the writing.

"My parents bought a house on Fireweed

Island? They're moving here? Oh. My. Gosh." I looked over at Nick, who was trying to gauge my reaction. "Is Muppet coming?"

"I think that's the plan."

"How long have you known about this?" I asked, smiling.

"They wanted to surprise you and your sister, so they've been working with me and a realtor I know to find this place."

"Is it a second house?" I asked.

"They already sold their house in Illinois. That's actually why they're on a cruise. All of their items are in a long haul truck on the way here, and they needed a place to be."

"How in the world?"

"They like me." He smirked. "What can I say? I have that effect on people. I wanted to tell you, but . . ."

"No, this is good. This is actually really good. I'm glad you didn't tell me. It bypassed all the worrying and we just got to the end result. My family, as eccentric as they might be, will be close."

"Really?"

I nodded.

"Yeah. I'm glad they're moving here."

Nick let out a deep sigh. "Thank God." He rubbed my shoulders. "I did, however, put them on the other side of the island."

I laughed. "See? We are a perfect match. Does my sister know?"

"I don't think so. They're arriving on the 28th."

"Of December?"

Nick laughed.

"I think I'll save that for after she gets back, or she might want to stay on Hound Island." I ran my hand along the bed. "I just can't believe how beautiful this is. I'll never want to leave."

"That was by design."

"Is that so?"

He nodded, a familiar gleam in his eye.

"Well, would you like to open one of your gifts? It's nothing this extravagant," I told him, suddenly feeling kind of sheepish.

"You are my present."

"And you just know the right thing to say."

He slid his hand into mine, and I led him into the family room. I found the package I was looking for under the tree and handed it to him.

I drew a deep breath as he unwrapped the small box and opened the lid.

He unfolded the piece of paper and looked up at me.

"Reservations for New Year's Eve?" he asked.

"Sophie said you liked this ski resort—"

Nick swooped me into his arms, kissing me as my body melted into him. I thought back to the first night we met and how much had changed, but also how much had stayed the same. He still made me weak in the knees and could make my world spin just from one look.

"So you like it?" I asked.

"I love it." He slid his tongue along his bottom lip, and it took all my willpower not to keep kissing him. "When did you make this reservation?"

"The day after we picked out the Christmas tree."

His smile covered his entire face. "Well, that explains why it was booked."

"What do you mean?"

He slid his phone out of his pocket and showed me an email.

"I called to make a reservation, but they said someone had just snagged the last room. They put me on the wait list."

"You're kidding."

He shook his head. "You beat me to the punch."

I saw a set of car lights pull into my driveway, and I glanced at Nick.

"Recognize the car?"

Nick craned his neck and nodded.

"Who is it?" I asked.

"You'll just have to wait to see."

I smacked him playfully, but he pulled me into his arms and didn't let go.

I kept my gaze firmly planted out the window, wondering who in the world might be showing up on Christmas Eve.

A woman climbed out of the car and reached inside for a large bag. She closed the door and looked toward my cabin. I didn't recognize her and wondered if I was supposed to.

As she got closer, I saw a familiarity that was impossible to ignore.

"Is that your mom?" I asked.

"She didn't think she'd be able to get off work and didn't know until today."

"What does she do?" I asked.

"She's a nurse." He looked into my eyes. "I didn't mean to spring this on you, but I didn't want you to worry, and since I didn't know for sure—"

"I'm not worried. I'm excited. I can't wait to meet the woman who brought you into the world."

I flung open the door and Nick's mom smiled.

"Aren't you the cutest thing in the world?" she asked as Nick took her bag away. "I'm Alma. You must be Holly."

"That's me."

The warmth radiating from Nick's mom showed me the apple didn't roll very far from the tree. It also told me everything I experienced with Nick was genuine, and I didn't know how in the world I got so lucky.

Alma gave me a long squeeze, and when Nick was out of earshot, she whispered, "Thank you for showing my son another way."

She let go of me and hugged Nick while I stood in amazement.

Moving to Fireweed had been the best thing I'd ever done.

I was standing at my window, watching the snow swirl to the ground. It was a little after one o'clock in the morning. Nick's mom was across the street at his house, and Nick was down the hall, getting ready for bed.

We'd all gone to a midnight service, and once it had ended, the snow started to fall. My sister texted me that Santa was spotted south of us, along with some photos of the farm. It was gorgeous. The entire farm was lit up with Christmas lights, and where she was staying looked right up my sister's alley.

I took a sip of hot cider and felt Nick come up behind me.

"God, you're a beautiful creature to see," Nick said, draping his arms over my shoulders.

"I think I like how this feels." I wiggled my

back into him.

"I know I do." He took the cup away and put it on the table.

I turned around and laid my head on his chest as he held me tightly.

"I have to tell you something," he whispered, and my body stilled.

"Is everything okay?" I asked, feeling his warm breath scatter across my head.

"I know I want to marry you someday, Holly."

I lifted my head and our eyes met.

"I—"

"This isn't a proposal," he continued. "It's an explanation. I wanted my grandmother's wedding ring. She and my grandfather were married for sixty years. They did it right. My mom wasn't sure when she could come back out, so she brought it with her."

My heart was pounding and I was trying to keep my bearings.

"When my mom showed up tonight, I knew something was wrong."

"What do you mean?" I asked, worry running through me.

"The reason my mom was able to get off work is because she's sick."

"What do you mean sick? How sick?"

"I noticed she was walking differently. She's stiffer, slower. I questioned her about it earlier and she told me everything was fine."

"But it's not fine?" I asked.

Pain darted through his gaze and he shook his head.

"When I got her settled in at my house, I questioned her again. She told me she was diagnosed with MS several years ago and didn't want to tell me. My mom thought by now they would've found a medicine or a cocktail of drugs that would have slowed its progression, but now she's not as confident. I guess it's been creeping up on her, and she's not sure how much longer she'll be able to work. Financially, she's fine." He bit his lip. "She's got a large savings."

"But physically . . ." My voice trailed off.

The swell of emotion in my chest was painful, gutting, as I saw the worry in Nick's gaze.

"I just wish she would have told me."

I nodded, feeling the sadness running through him.

"The medicines have improved greatly, but they haven't found the right combination for her yet."

"They will." I nodded, trying to be reassuring.

"She's lost a lot of strength in her grip, and she's dropped several things at the hospital she works at. I'm not sure how much longer she's going to be able to work."

"I'm so sorry," I whispered.

"I didn't want to tell you tonight, but I wanted you to know." He let out a deep breath. "And it feels so good just having someone to tell."

"I'm here for however you need me," I assured him, wrapping my arms around his waist. "I know I can't fix this or make things okay . . ."

He pulled me in tightly, and I sucked in a deep breath.

"Thank you, baby," he whispered, and I felt the sting of tears. "You make things more than okay." He held me tighter. "I just love you so much, Holly. I don't think you know how much you've changed my life."

"I feel the same." I took a deep breath, inhaling everything about the man I loved so deeply.

"You tempted me with a life I never thought I wanted."

"You tempted me, period." I giggled.

"Just don't lose that light."

"I'll try not to," I promised.

"That's what I needed to hear." He smiled.

"Do you want to open another present?"

"Should I?" he asked, and I took a step back.

"I would if I were you." I wiggled my brows and he laughed. "Might take your mind off things."

"Then how can I say no?"

"Okay, hopefully, I don't fall over myself getting to the tree." The only light was the glow from the Christmas tree, which made things a little dangerous.

"We could just turn on the lights," Nick suggested, taking a seat on my favorite chair.

"And ruin the mood lighting? No way." I dug through the packages, found the one I was looking for, and handed it to him.

"I don't know whether to be excited or nervous." He began untying the bows on the small package, and I couldn't hide my smile as I sat on the floor in front of him.

"This has to be the coolest tool belt I've ever

seen."

"I was excited to find it, but look in the pouch," I told him.

He dug his hand inside and pulled out a red negligée.

"You never stop tempting me." Nick smiled, and I grabbed the red lace.

"Remember how I said I had a few fantasies?"

His eyes darkened, and he scooted forward in the chair.

"Well, one of them has to do with that tool belt and this little thing." I stood up and straddled him on the chair, but he lifted me up.

"No, you don't," he warned as I wrapped my legs around his waist. "This time, we're doing it my way."

"Ooh. This sounds good." I smiled, nuzzling into his neck.

"If things get really crazy, we can whip out the zip ties." He chuckled.

"It's like you can read my mind," I teased.

Nick carried me and the tool belt into my bedroom while I clutched the red lace. He placed me on the bed, pulled off his shirt, and got out of his pants, strapping the belt around his waist.

"You're actually doing it," I squealed. "I can't believe it."

"Why wouldn't I?" He smiled, his gaze falling to the red lace.

"But I want all the way." My eyes narrowed on him and his smile grew.

"Fine." He pulled off his boxers and my heart nearly exploded. Even when something was silly and unexpected, he managed to make it look sexy.

"Yours is easy to put on," I told him, slipping out of my clothes.

"Then let me help," he said, unfastening my bra while sprinkling kisses across my skin and slinking the lace over my head.

"That works nicely. Maybe I'll always have you dress me."

"I wouldn't mind." He slid me up the bed, taking in every inch of me and making me feel like I was the most gorgeous woman to walk this planet.

"Best Christmas Eve ever," I said, circling my arms around Nick and bringing him close.

"I couldn't agree more," he whispered, bringing his mouth to mine.

Feeling the stroke of his tongue as our kisses deepened sent me into another orbit as I imagined getting to spend the rest of my life with him. Everything meant so much more now, and I didn't even understand why. He hadn't asked me to marry him, but knowing we were both wanting a future together made this moment even more special. It made this Christmas feel more permanent, the memories more important.

Nick's hands drifted underneath the lace, scattering goose bumps with each stroke of his hand, his mouth following and sending a wave of chills through me. The leather tool belt dug into my skin, and I had to smile as I ran my fingers along the edge until I found the buckle.

Another one of my bright ideas.

I unfastened it and tossed the belt on the ground. His eyes connected with mine, and the heated expression running through his gaze made my entire body respond to his. I moved my hips toward him and he smiled, placing soft kisses down my breasts to my belly.

His mouth trailed down my stomach as he shoved the lace up, fueling my desire. He teased and taunted me with his tongue going lower and lower until he nudged open my legs. I felt his hot breath along my thighs as my fingers coiled through his hair, savoring every single second of what he was giving but not wanting it to end.

"Kiss me," I whispered.

Coaxing him up gently, he tugged the lace over my head and leaned over me, his mouth crashing to mine. I slowly trailed my fingers down his back, feeling the curves of his tight body as he slowly worked his knees between mine.

He cupped my behind, bringing my knee up as he entered, and my entire world spun into ecstasy as I ground my hips into him with each thrust, the heat rolling off his body as his fingers worked lower and in unison. He kissed me hard, and I felt my entire world surrender to his.

His breathing quickened, and I buried my mouth into his arm as the first cry of ecstasy escaped my lips. The sound made him respond by burying deeper, his heart pounding as he propped himself on his elbow and slowly brought down my leg.

"I love you," he whispered next to my ear, and I wiggled into his body still propped against mine.

"I might love you more," I confessed.

"Wanna make a bet?" he teased.

It was a perfect ending to a perfect day.

I curled into his body and felt our breathing slow as we fell asleep in a bed full of more love than I ever thought possible.

Morning came before I was ready, but waking up next to Nick was the best Christmas present ever. The way his arms draped over my waist and his chin nuzzled into the crook of my neck spelled nothing but happiness for me.

Hearing his steady breaths made my world complete. I looked out the window and saw that several inches of snow had come down overnight. It was the perfect Christmas.

"Merry Christmas," he whispered, and my entire body melted into his.

"Merry Christmas."

He stretched, and I turned over to see how cute he was in the morning. His short, dark hair was a flat and tangled mess. He flashed a sleepy smile.

"Waking up with you feels good. You feel so right in my arms," he said, his voice gruffer than usual.

"Don't be so surprised," I teased. "I knew it all along."

"Is that so?" He pulled me deeper into him.

"Very so," I said, giggling, as we lay tangled in the comforter. "I guess we should get up. I don't want your mom to think we stay in bed all day."

"She's a late sleeper. I doubt she'll be up for

another hour or so."

I twisted myself into a sheet and pulled it off the bed with me as I went to shut the curtains.

"Just in case." I wriggled my brows.

"I could get used to waking up with you every morning."

"There are a lot of things I could get used to," I hollered, hopping in the shower.

Nick came in to brush his teeth, and something popped into my head.

"You know, if your mom needs to move closer to you someday, I'm guessing there might be a cabin available in the future." I wiped the water off the shower glass, and Nick's eyes connected with mine. "And I'd be more than happy to have her live here. It would make me happy."

"What are you saying?" he asked. He was only in a pair of boxers, and it made my heart happy.

"I'm saying if she ever needs more care, this cabin would be perfect. It's light, bright, and cheery. If what you said last night is true, I might not be living here for decades to come. That's all I'm saying."

"Oh, it's true. I'm not letting you get away." Seeing the love and relief flash through his gaze made me want a repeat of last night. "But you'd do that for my mom? There are plenty of rental properties on the island."

"I can't imagine not doing it." I shook my head. "Things always happen for a reason. We can't predict the future, but we can certainly live right in the present."

"My life can't get any more right with you in

it."

"I feel the same way, Nick." I dried off and stepped out of the shower.

Nicks eyes fastened on mine, and he came over, sweeping me into his arms. My bare body pressed into his, and I knew there wasn't another place I'd rather be.

Chapter Twenty-Four

"**Y**ou know what I think?" I hollered into the hotel suite and didn't bother waiting for a response. "I think we should up the ante on the whole Polar Bear Dip."

I pulled the tie around the robe and glanced in the mirror. Nick had surprised me for my birthday and brought me to the same hotel where we'd spent New Year's. It was tucked away in the mountains, yet it had everything a person could possibly need.

I walked out of the bedroom and took in a sleepy yawn. I thought Fireweed was relaxing, but this place took it one step further. It was a perfect February escape. We woke up this morning to a couple's massage, breakfast in the village, and shopping, but now it was my turn to surprise Nick.

"What do you think?" I called to Nick. "Ready for my idea about the Polar Bear Dip?"

I scanned the small living room and kitchenette, not seeing him. I'd been in the shower, but he didn't say anything about leaving.

"Nick?" I asked. The curtains leading to our private Jacuzzi patio were closed, so he wasn't outside.

Just as I was about to call for him again, I heard the keycard in the door. He swung open the door carrying a plate full of chocolate covered strawberries.

"My favorite," I gushed as he gave me a quick kiss. "So you didn't hear my idea about the Polar Bear Dip."

"No, I didn't." He grinned, setting the strawberries on the counter in the kitchenette.

"I think we need to do a Polar Bear Dip with some real gusto." I smiled, but he pulled me into him.

"I thought that dip was pretty perfect," he countered. "And the library even got more books."

I giggled and pulled away. I grabbed the stereo remote and turned on music. His eyes followed me as I slowly walked toward the bedroom but stopped just outside.

"Come on." I wiggled my finger, and a worried look darted through his gaze.

"We have reservations," he said, almost stuttering.

"This is more important." I smiled, cranking

up the tunes. "It's time for a Polar Bear Skinny Dip."

I dropped my robe, and his eyes became heated with want as I stepped toward him.

"Holly," he whispered as I wrapped myself around him.

"What do you say?" I asked, taking a step back. "Ready to try the skinny dip version?"

I wiggled my naked hips, ran my hands down my sides, and gave a little bounce, and he sucked in a jagged breath, but it wasn't until I reached for the curtain to the patio that he nearly tackled me to the floor.

It was a soft landing, but completely unexpected as the curtain rod bounced to the ground and the fabric fell to the floor.

"What the heck?" I asked, his body curled around mine as if a bomb was about to go off. I glanced toward the sliding patio door and saw a row of shoes.

"I swear to God, you're going to keep me on my toes for the rest of my life." He laughed, his body still covering mine.

"What are you talking about?" I asked, his embrace only tightening.

"Surprise!" I heard our group of friends yell out at the top of their lungs.

"Surprise," Nick echoed, still on top of me.

"Oh. My. Gosh. I just flashed my friends," I groaned.

"No, no. I'm pretty sure I got you in time," he said, still covering me up.

But I wasn't so sure . . . timing and all.

I heard Sophie instructing everyone through the glass door to turn around, and my heart sped up mightily with embarrassment.

"So maybe we'll try the skinny dipping another time," I whispered, my cheeks flaming.

"I honestly don't know why it didn't occur to me that this could happen." Nick grinned and craned his neck behind him to make sure our friends had all turned around.

He rolled off me and reached for the robe, draping it over me as he helped me up.

I tied the robe around me and laughed, giving Nick a huge kiss.

I glanced out the slider to see the snow on the patio surrounding our friends and the steam from the hot tub rolling into the air.

"This was quite the surprise," I joked, tapping on the glass, and everyone turned around.

"It turned into quite the doozey."

I noticed Sophie, Natty, and Jewels bunched together and still not turning around.

"We should probably let them in. How long have they been outside?" I asked, noticing Tori looking a little blue.

"Since you were in the shower." He slid open the slider, and the girls turned around, holding a street sign that read *Holly Lane.*

I glanced at Nick, who was beaming. "I petitioned the state, then the island, then the town. You no longer live on State Road 26. Our road has been officially changed to Holly Lane."

"You can do that?" I asked.

"Apparently so." He smiled, hugging me as

everyone piled inside, laughing and talking excitedly, wishing me happy birthday and almost making the other mishap blend into obscurity.

"Happy Birthday," Sophie said, giving me a big hug. "We didn't see a thing."

"Not a thing," Natty said, nodding.

"Well, we might have seen a little." Tori pinched her fingers together. "But it all happened so fast, I'm not even sure any of us know what we saw."

"What time are the reservations, Nick?" Sophie asked, trying to soften the blow.

"Fewer than ten minutes, actually. I think we might be late." Nick glanced at me still standing in my robe.

"I can hurry," I promised him, but Sophie shook her head.

"Don't rush. You're the birthday girl. We'll go downstairs to the restaurant and check in."

She gave me a quick hug and ushered everyone out of our suite.

Nick laughed and glanced toward the patio. "I think I need to come up with lots of plan Bs."

"What do you mean?" I asked.

He looped his hand in mine and pulled me outside.

The crisp air took my breath away, but the snow-covered mountains surrounding us were so beautiful I didn't care.

"So I just can't wait any longer," he began, and my eyes fell to the hot tub.

"You want to do the skinny dip after all?" I asked.

271

"Everything you do is so damn cute." He grinned.

"Is that a problem?"

"Not a problem but a definite complication, especially if we're supposed to get things done in this world."

"Like what?" I asked.

"Like asking you to marry me."

Nick kneeled in front of me and reached for my hand.

"Holly, I wanted to make your birthday one you'd never forget because you've made every one of my days unforgettable since you came dancing into it. I wake up in the morning excited to hear about your dreams, I look forward to finishing work so we can watch eighties movies together, I dream up things I can do to surprise you, and yet you always outdo me. You always manage to surprise me."

Nick's eyes stayed on mine and my entire world went into slow motion. He reached into his back pocket and pulled out a tiny ring box. My heart sputtered in delight.

"I can't wait to spend the rest of our lives together, Holly Wildes. I know sharing a life with you will mean a dull ride will never exist, and I can't wait for it. You challenge me and make me excited for each day."

I slid my hands across my cheeks, wiping away the tears of joy.

"Holly, will you marry me?" he asked.

I nodded my head and fell to my knees, the snow soaking through my bathrobe as he slipped the ring on my finger.

"Yes, I'll marry you," I said. "A million times over, I'll marry you."

"You've finally given me what I was looking for and didn't even know it," Nick whispered. "You've given me a new way to look at the same old things."

"I love you, Nick," I whispered.

"I love you more," he teased.

"Wanna bet?"

"Always."

I never imagined when I moved to Fireweed Island that my life would be forever changed, but as I looked at the man I'd fallen so deeply in love with, I knew this had always been in the plan. I was just lucky enough to find the right path to him, and for once, I didn't get stuck on one of life's detours.

Keep reading for an excerpt from

Mia

A Luke Fletcher and V Mafia Novel

Chapter One

Mia

"Come on, Mia. You can do this," Ginger Mesnet coaxed me. She shook her head full of blonde curls as she climbed up the steps with her black stilettos clacking.

I looked up the long flight of marble stairs that threatened to carry me straight to hell. Granted, it was a hell I chose, but I didn't expect things to feel so wrong once I arrived.

On the surface, the idea sounded like a good one, possibly even fun. Enjoy a night of drinks, meet a few good-looking men, and help out my brother, Luke.

Luke owned one of the largest private security firms in the country. Celebrities and politicians regularly tapped his company for services that law enforcement couldn't provide. He also specialized in countersurveillance and risk management, which often meant being proactive when it came to the bad guys, which was what led me here tonight.

My brother's line of work often put him in complex situations with outcomes bordering on downright dangerous. Thankfully for him, he managed to run into the right woman who was about as twisted as he was, and they both loved the adventure of it. In fewer than two weeks, they'd be walking down the aisle, and because of that, I volunteered to keep an eye on someone for my brother so Luke could spend a blissful three weeks away from work.

My preference? I tended to enjoy a paintbrush and a blank canvas rather than sneaking down an alley to spy on someone, but here I was in all my sparkly glamor.

I think my willingness to help my brother out was because his relationship with Hannah had secretly given me hope that screwed-up people could find love. Plus, he'd caught me in a weak moment. I'd just broken up with another quasi-boyfriend before coming to New York. I seemed to specialize in men who were as walled off as me. Usually, it was a win-win.

Regardless, I now stood at the entrance to a singles event in the middle of Manhattan with a gallery owner I didn't want to disappoint and a mission to spy on someone for my brother, of whom I'd only seen a photo.

I watched Ginger tread up the stairs as a group of men, with satin and feathers wrapped around their heads, meandered up the steps.

Was this what my life had come to?

Why, yes. I think it had.

"I don't hear your feet trying to catch up." Ginger's voice rang through the air as her red silk dress cascaded down the steps behind her.

One thing I learned about Ginger was that she lived for any type of affair that would allow her to dress up and drink, which was probably what made her the perfect owner of an art gallery. She was also the perfect unsuspecting companion for the night.

A woman with a black cape hopped up the stairs, and I kept in a groan.

Did I mention the singles event tonight was a masquerade ball? I guess that would explain the capes, masks, and feathers a little better. Truthfully, the idea of hiding behind a disguise seemed like a great idea yesterday.

Now?

Not so much.

It didn't provide nearly enough protection from the world I was about to enter.

It was like *Eyes Wide Shut* met a New York *Furry* Convention.

It didn't matter how much gold glitter I'd painted around my eyes. I didn't belong here. Where I did belong was back in my studio on the beach in California, painting to raging music and blissfully ignoring the outside world.

A man clad in a rented tuxedo zipped past me and glanced over his shoulder as I stood rethinking my life. His peacock mask made me cringe as his beady eyes stared back at me like I was a disgrace to singles everywhere.

I probably was. I didn't like dating, relationships, or any complication that involved emotion. I reserved those pesky feelings for the canvas.

The man hopped up the rest of the steps to join the other singles, and I debated whether I wanted to make a run for it. No client of my brother deserved this type of devotion. Besides, how would I know who was who with masks on everyone? As a team, we didn't think this through very clearly.

I sucked in a deep breath and glanced around. It was definitely time to get out of here. Ginger would have to forgive me, and so would my brother.

"Don't even think about getting out of here." A man's sultry voice snuck up on me from behind. He sounded like pure sex. The huskiness intrigued me, but I refused to turn around to give him what he wanted.

When I didn't acknowledge him, the man placed his fingers on the small of my back and an unexpected thrill spiked through me.

"What do you think you're doing?" I snapped, turning to face the guy who was beyond brazen, but instead of being angry, I was in awe of the man in front of me.

His icy blue eyes rested on mine as I studied him. His chiseled features looked like a carving from one of the masters, and he filled out his expensive suit to perfection. My eyes dropped to his pouty lips before bringing my gaze back to his, and that's when I realized how much he resembled the photo of Drake Volkov, the man I was supposed to be watching from a distance.

I stiffened at the realization but forced the worry away. There would be absolutely no reason for Drake to know anything about me or why I was here. Luke would've made sure of that.

I turned my gaze to the street below. My brother's instructions had been simple. Keep an eye on Drake from afar and find out who he was here with and where he was going after the event. By the looks of it, I'd say Drake Volkov was here alone.

"Well?" I asked again, attempting to sound annoyed. "I'm waiting for an answer."

Intrigue flashed through his eyes, and my pulse increased slightly. I'd never gotten nervous around men.

Ever.

In fact, I liked to believe I made them nervous. I'd always managed to maintain control of my life. Relationships had never been a priority, and they never would be. I didn't need a man to be satisfied. I had my work. I had a full life back in California. If I had needs, I made sure they were met and moved on.

"My hope is to convince a very beautiful woman to stay and endure the horrors of the evening with me. You don't belong here, and neither do I." The man could cast a spell with just his words, and they curled around me like magic.

"When you put it that way, why would I ever run away? Sounds like a delightful event." I couldn't hide my smile, but a pulse of worry dashed through my veins. "If you can tell me one good reason to stay at an event with a bunch of men in feathers, then maybe I'll reconsider."

"Because I'm not one of them." His eyes

glinted with satisfaction, and I had to chuckle.

Drake was confident and smooth, two characteristics that usually got me in deep trouble.

"Which reminds me. How did you get away with wearing no mask to a masquerade ball?" My brow arched.

"I'm not much for rules," he replied simply as he held out his arm for me, and rather than run away, I slipped mine through his.

Drake slowly led me up the stairs, and I had to remind myself that he was completely off-limits and the man my brother wanted me to tail.

"What made you come tonight if you're dreading it as much as me?" I glanced at him and noticed the dark stubble along his jawline. This guy was beyond sexy and definitely my kind of trouble.

"I'm here on a dare. How about you?" he answered.

I let go of his arm and glanced toward the crowd of people congregating near the bar. I didn't see Ginger, which wasn't a surprise. She managed to get swallowed into whatever affair she was attending.

"I wish I could say the same." I smiled and saw a number of women slow their steps purely to admire how handsome this guy was. I couldn't say I blamed them. Besides, he wasn't mine to claim.

"There you are," Ginger said, rushing over with a martini in her hand. "There are men all over the place." She barely gave a glance in

Drake's direction. "How about we move toward the dance floor?"

"I'm not feeling much like dancing," I confessed.

Noticing Ginger's expression fall, I quickly changed my tactic. After all, I didn't want to blow my chances at her art gallery because I'd brought her here under false pretenses. In Ginger's eyes, I was here to find a date for my brother's wedding.

"Maybe it's just my nerves. He's already caught me trying to escape once." I pointed my thumb in Drake's direction, but she didn't bother to look at him.

"It's true. Really, you should be thanking me that she's still here." His low voice held an intensity that unsteadied me. I wasn't used to this kind of reaction. I always knew how to keep a safe distance between desire, need, and lust, but as I stood here next to him, the line was starting to blur. Maybe it was because I knew he was off-limits. That had to be it. I knew I couldn't have him, so I wanted him even more.

Made sense.

I snuck a look at Drake, but his eyes were already fastened on mine. His gaze was filled with some sort of possession I'd never encountered before, and it sent an unexpected shiver through me.

"Umm . . ." I bit my lip, completely taken aback at my response. I was rendered speechless.

I was never rendered speechless. I always had too much to say about everything and everyone.

"Let's get you a drink and get you loosened

up." Ginger pulled me with her before I could gather my thoughts or object.

I felt Drake's eyes on me all the way to the bar, and I was quite tempted to give him another look, but I resisted.

"So you can thank me later for pulling you away from the most notorious bachelor in all of Hell's Kitchen." Ginger laughed nervously. "Not to mention, he's the son of a mobster. Not wedding date material."

I leaned against the bar and tapped my fingers along the white marble as I waited impatiently to place my drink order. Leave it to my brother to skip one or two important details before sending me here.

"That doesn't automatically make him bad," I whispered, thinking back to my own rather cavalier ideas about relationships and sex. I liked having zero commitment. And as far as family not always sticking to the right side of the law, I wasn't one to judge. Not all of our family was on the right side of the bars.

"What's his name, anyway?" I asked casually, pretending to play the part my brother assigned.

Ginger's loose blonde curls bounced along her shoulders as she broke into laughter.

"Drake Volkov. But I'm telling you, if you knew even half of his issues, you'd stay far away." She continued to shake her head. "Just trust me. You don't want a thing to do with that man or his family." Her eyes narrowed on me as she took a sip of her drink and I ordered mine.

"I mean it," she continued. "Steer clear. The

entire family should be locked up."

Obviously, Ginger didn't know me that well, or she'd understand that the moment someone told me not to do something was the exact moment I wanted to do it.

It was a sick trait, but I couldn't help it.

I glanced behind me to where Drake had been standing, but he was nowhere to be seen. I'd found him and already managed to let him slip away. This kind of work really was exhausting.

I reached for my glass of champagne and took a sip. By the looks of the place, I'd need several glasses to survive the night.

I slid my finger along my hair and readjusted the mask around my eyes. Gold glitter floated through the air, and I held in a groan of frustration.

My brother owed me big time.

"There are two very good-looking men over by the sign-in table, and they're looking our way," Ginger hummed, setting her empty glass on a table.

I followed her gaze and saw two decent-looking guys watching us as they drank beer. Granted, they were wearing masks, so who knew, but neither did a thing for me.

In fact, the red velvet curtains behind them looked far more appealing—especially from an artist's point of view—but I knew I had to tread lightly with Ginger. After a two-year court battle, her divorce was finalized one month ago, and she hasn't wasted a moment since.

Not to mention, we were two nights away

from my big night, the opening of my exhibit at her gallery. She held the key to my entrance into the New York art scene, and if it meant some harmless flirting, so be it.

One of the guys held up his beer toward us, which was exactly the opening Ginger had been waiting for. She let out an excited chirp, and I held my glass tighter, praying it would shatter in my fingertips and buy me a bloody ticket out of here.

"You know you don't want to bother with either of those men," Drake said in a hushed tone. His voice made my skin sizzle with excitement. "They won't interest you in the least bit."

Ginger snapped her head to look at the man standing behind me. Her gaze hardened on him, and I realized in that moment that there might be more than one reason Drake was off-limits. I turned around to see him but took a step back.

"And you will?" I asked, folding my one arm across my chest.

I took a sip of champagne, not taking my eyes off him.

"Guaranteed."

The attraction I felt toward Drake was insanely dangerous. The combination of dark hair and light blue eyes was hauntingly beautiful, and the dark lashes outlining his eyes would probably be the death of me. Men like this didn't exist where I lived in California. I was used to the surfer boys and club owners. This guy had an edge about him that drew me in far too deep.

"Certainly sure of yourself," I retorted, swallowing more champagne.

"If I don't believe in myself, no one else will. It's totally your call, though. If you're into those two over there, be my guest. I'll just hang at the bar, enjoying the view of you in that goddess of a dress."

The cocky bastard had me. He could read me like an open book, and I didn't like it one bit.

Not one bit.

I hadn't stayed single this long by falling for some guy's pick-up lines and . . .

Who the hell was I kidding?

He was the exact type of guy I ran from, but for some reason, I didn't want to go anywhere, which was a danger sign as clear as any.

I couldn't be a part of whatever Drake had planned for the rest of the evening, or I wouldn't get the information Luke needed. I brought my eyes back to his, and he looked thoroughly amused.

"Listen, I'm looking for safe with no drama, so I'll take my chances with the Hardy Boys over there." I kept my face void of expression and pointed at the two guys who were still watching us closely.

Ginger snickered, and I suddenly felt bad for Drake, but he didn't miss a beat.

"Well, it sounds like the matchup is off to a good start already. If you change your mind, you'll know where to find me." He turned around but stopped and spun back around. "And don't let Ginger taint your views about me too much.

She's biased."

Ginger grabbed my hand and nearly pulled my arm off as she tugged me toward the two men.

"So you know him?" I asked. "Like personally? Not just his reputation."

She let out a sigh and slowed her pace.

"My sister was married to his brother."

Chapter Two

Drake

"Damn," I muttered under my breath.

Watching this goddess of a woman glide across the ballroom with Ginger was almost more than I could handle as a gentleman.

Hell.

Who was I kidding? I was no gentleman. Never had been.

Seeing her hips sway underneath the gold sequins made it difficult to look decent in a room full of people. I leaned against the bar and ordered water without taking my eyes off her. Her dark brown hair skimmed her bronze shoulders, and her body language told me she was confident and in control, yet there was a perfectly imperfect quality about her that drew me in. I pictured myself undressing her and . . .

She threw her head back and laughter followed. I didn't like that another man was making her laugh.

I took a sip of water and stared at the marble

bar. Maybe I'd guessed wrong about her. Maybe the Hardy Boys were her type. Maybe she liked preppy guys who belonged to country clubs and wanted wives to be seen and not heard.

I shook my head, not believing it for a second.

I brought my eyes back to her and watched as she slid her hands along her sides. She took a sip of her champagne but then froze, quickly dropping her eyes to the floor. Something had changed.

I stiffened, and my gaze darted to the men in front of her. Did one of them say something to make her uncomfortable? My heart rate started beating rapidly as I watched her shake her head and take a step back. The blond one moved toward her to close the gap between them. He grabbed her wrist, which she shook free, but then he grabbed it again. The room fell away around me as my eyes narrowed on this prick.

Ginger wasn't even paying attention as she chatted up his buddy, and my pulse spiked.

Typical Ginger.

The woman cocked her head and shook it again. I took in a ragged breath and saw the creep slowly slide his hand along her waist, narrowing the space between them as he moved his fingers along her waist. She grabbed his hand and shoved it away, but the jerk went for her again. This time, he pulled her body flush against his and fire ran through my veins.

Nothing else mattered but forcing this scum to kiss the floor she walked on. My fingers tingled with the opportunity to make him pay as I darted through the crowd, sailing past anyone in my way as I closed in on this predator.

He said something else to her, and before I even reached them, she took the guy's hand back in hers and smiled wickedly.

Wickedly.

It wasn't until the man dropped to his knees that I realized she'd bent his thumb backward.

I stopped in my tracks and backed into the crowd, unable to keep my eyes off her. She was mesmerizing, in control, and sexy as hell. My core tensed just watching her. I'd wanted to come to her rescue—be her knight in shining armor—but she didn't need rescuing. This woman didn't need to be saved, and certainly not by someone like me. I wiped my forehead and shook my head.

Hell. Who was I kidding?

I couldn't even save myself.

While I stood in awe, she finished off her champagne and looked at the man on the floor with indifference as he climbed back to his feet. He rubbed his hand and glared at her.

I scanned the ballroom and realized not a single person—including Ginger—even realized what had happened.

I threw my gaze back in her direction and saw her looking back at me. My pulse soared and my body instantly responded to her.

I needed to stay away from her. I had work to do tonight and she would only add complication. A slight curl touched her lips, and my chest tightened. I wanted her. There was no getting around it.

She slowly walked in my direction but passed right on by on her way to the bar.

This woman was a marvel.

I watched the bartender flirt with her, and she seemed extremely receptive, which I found unnerving.

No.

It wasn't the flirting that was unnerving. It was that I gave a damn.

She glanced in my direction and her smile widened.

What was it she wanted?

My eyes raked along her body, and I hardened immediately thinking about what I wanted to do to her. I didn't have time for this. I turned around and worked my way through the crowd toward the dance floor, but her voice followed me.

"You free the rest of the night?" she asked.

I stopped. I detected a thread of hopefulness in her words and held in a silent sigh. I didn't want to do what I was about to do, but it was better for all involved.

"Actually, no." I turned around and smelled the sweetness of champagne.

She'd removed her mask, and my world dropped out from under me. She parted her mouth and slowly ran her tongue along her pink lips. I didn't know if she was doing it on purpose or if she honestly had no idea what she was doing to me. I lifted my gaze from her lips back to her almond shaped eyes, and I knew I was about to do something I'd regret.

"But I am free for the next while." I glanced at my Rolex and she laughed, catching me off-guard.

"What?" I asked, my brows pinching together.

"People still wear watches?" She grinned, and my heart nearly doubled in size.

Not good. I wasn't supposed to have one of those.

"If they want to get places on time. Yeah, they're handy devices," I shot back, and she giggled.

Yes, giggled . . . I'd never heard a sound so addicting in my life.

"That's what phones are for." She steadied her eyes on mine, and I saw her struggling internally with something. A few seconds of silence passed before she took a step closer to me and placed her hand on my arm. "Is there somewhere we can get some fresh air?"

For some reason, I was struck speechless, so I pointed toward a row of French doors that led to a terrace. It overlooked several dilapidated brick buildings that developers hadn't gotten their hands on yet, but maybe at night, it wouldn't be as bad.

"Good. That's the direction Ginger went, so maybe I can find her. I want to let her know I'm leaving soon." She dropped her hand and started toward the doors.

She spotted Ginger and made her way over while I stayed put. Ginger nodded and gave her a quick hug.

The woman slid through the crowd and

motioned for me to follow her before she pushed open the door. A cold blast of air blew inside.

"You sure you want to be out here? It's kind of cold," I asked, coming up behind her.

The dress stretched over her hips, and I fought reaching out for her. The jerk ruined things for me tonight, but probably not as much as for the woman in front of me.

"Can't handle it?" she teased, bringing me out of my fog.

"Oh, I can handle it," I assured her as she walked onto the empty balcony.

Her dress caught the lights from above and shimmered in all the right places. She turned around quickly and caught me checking out her ass.

Damn.

I usually had more tact than that, but I swore I saw a hint of a smile tug at her lips.

"What's your name?" I questioned, loosening my tie.

"Doesn't matter," she said softly. "I don't live here. I live in California, and after tonight's turn of events, I can't wait to get back."

I let out a deep sigh and shook my head in disgust.

"I'm sorry that guy tainted your trip. New York's not a bad place. Usually, people just stick to themselves and go about their business." I leaned sideways against the metal railing and watched her carefully. There was something about the way she brushed things off that told me this wasn't the first time she'd had to take care of herself. The thought angered me as I drew in a quiet breath and looked over the still-bustling city below.

"It didn't tarnish it. I like New York, always have. I'm just tired and . . ."

I brought my eyes back to her, and she bit her lip.

"I wish it had been me who dropped that guy to his knees," I said as if that would matter.

"Is that so?" She arched one of her dark brows, and I knew she could drop me to mine with just one look.

I nodded.

"I actually wanted to thank you before I left." She took a step closer and licked her bottom lip.

"For what? I didn't do anything." I shook my head.

"I saw you coming over." She twisted her lips into a frown. "I recognized the look in your eyes."

"Look in my eyes?"

"From my brother," she answered. "I recognized that look from my brother when I was younger. Right before he was about to do some real damage, I'd see the same thing flash through his gaze."

"Sounds like my kind of guy." I laughed, seeing genuine appreciation flicker through her eyes.

"He's not really a people person." She chuckled, and the tension she'd been holding in seemed to lessen with his mention.

"Anyway, I'm going to exit this fine event because I have a hectic schedule for the next few days, but again, thank you. It's nice to know there's still decency in this world."

I'd seldom been called decent, and the comparison surprised me.

"I think anyone would have done the same."

"But they didn't." She turned around and walked away without another look in my direction.

Sign up for Karice's Newsletter to receive exclusive FREE novellas, new release information, and contests at

www.karicebolton.com
or follow her on
Facebook/Instagram/Pinterest/Twitter
@KariceBolton

BOOKS BY KARICE BOLTON

Romantic Suspense

LUKE FLETCHER SERIES

HIDDEN SINS

BURIED SINS

REDEMPTION

MIA

V MAFIA SERIES

BLAKE – FALL 2016

DEVIN – Coming Soon

JAXSON – Coming Soon

Contemporary Romance

ISLAND COUNTY SERIES

FINDING LOVE IN FORGOTTEN COVE

LOVE REDONE IN HIDDEN HARBOR

TANLGED LOVE ON PELICAN POINT

FOREVER LOVE ON FIREWEED ISLAND

TEMPTING LOVE ON HOLLY LANE

BEYOND LOVE SERIES

BEYOND CONTROL

BEYOND DOUBT

BEYOND REASON

BEYOND INTENT

BEYOND CHANCE

BEYOND PROMISE

BEYOND the MISTLETOE

Paranormal Romance

AFTERWORLD SERIES

Afterworld: Zombie RecruitZ

Afterworld: Zombie AlibiZ

Afterworld: Zombie UprisingZ

THE WITCH AVENUE SERIES

LONELY SOULS

ALTERED SOULS

RELEASED SOULS

SHATTERED SOULS

THE WATCHERS TRILOGY

AWAKENING

LEGIONS

CATACLYSM

TAKEN

ABOUT THE AUTHOR

Karice received an MFA in Creative Writing from the U of W. She has written close to thirty novels, and she has several exciting projects in the works (or at least she thinks they're exciting). Karice lives in the Pacific Northwest with her awesome husband and two cute English Bulldogs. She loves anything to do with snow, and she seeks out the stuff whenever she can, especially if there's a toasty fire to read by.

Made in the USA
Middletown, DE
10 July 2021